Books by Louise R. Innes

Contemporary Romance
Perfect Friends
Holiday Fling
Second Time Around
Forever Yours

Romantic Novellas
The New Year Resolution
The Love Formula

—•*A Daisy Thorne Mystery*•—

Death at Holly Lodge

LOUISE R. INNES

KENSINGTON
PUBLISHING CORP.

www.kensingtonbooks.com

KENSINGTON BOOKS are published by

Kensington Publishing Corp.
119 West 40th Street
New York, NY 10018

All Kensington titles, imprints, and distributed lines are available at special quantity discounts for bulk purchases for sales promotion, premiums, fund-raising, educational, or institutional use.

Special book excerpts or customized printings can also be created to fit specific needs. For details, write or phone the office of the Kensington Sales Manager: Attn.: Sales Department. Kensington Publishing Corp., 119 West 40th Street, New York, NY 10018. Phone: 1-800-221-2647.

The K logo is a trademark of Kensington Publishing Corp.

First Printing: October 2021
ISBN: 978-1-4967-2984-2

ISBN: 978-1-4967-2985-9 (ebook)

10 9 8 7 6 5 4 3 2 1

Printed in the United States of America

For Ed. You will be missed.

Chapter 1

Daisy sang along to a Christmas song as she pulled into the gravel driveway outside Holly Lodge. December was her favorite time of year. There was something magical in the air. Christmas trees twinkled in front windows, festive music flowed out of the shops, and everybody was in a joyous mood.

She parked between Floria's racing-green MINI Cooper and a dirty, white van with a building company logo on the side. The sliding side door was open, displaying an assortment of tools, boxes, and a folded-up ladder. Renovations were in full swing.

She turned off the radio and climbed out of the car, her feet crunching on the frosty ground. Holly Lodge was a Georgian-style family house that had once been rather grand, but had fallen into disrepair. She gazed up at the crumbling golden-brick exterior, admiring how it glowed in the weak, midmorning sun. The entrance was framed by rambling roses, which would be glorious in season, but were now a tangle of thorny twigs. Paint peeled off the front door, the porch looked worn and bare, and the windows were dirty and cracked. Only the holly bushes, after which the house had been named, seemed to thrive. Dark green and ripe with little red berries, they lined the drive and surrounded the front of the property.

Daisy breathed in the fresh country air as she took in the surroundings. A patchwork of green fields stretched out before her. In the distance was a hazy wood and beyond that, rolling purple hills. Holly Lodge was situated between Edgemead, where Daisy lived, and the village of Cobham. Once a hunting lodge, it was only accessible by a single narrow lane, flanked on either side by a deep ditch, overgrown foliage and then, endless meadows. In summer, they'd be filled with grazing cows and sheep from the nearby farm, but right now they were empty. Somewhere in the background, a stream tinkled.

"Daisy, you made it!" Floria, her best friend, dashed out of the house and flung her arms around her. "Come inside, Mimi's dying to see you."

Daisy hugged her, then followed her inside and into a large entrance hall. "Wow." She gazed up at the high ceiling from which hung a grubby, but intricate chandelier. The walls were adorned with period features and elaborate cornices that would be lovely if they weren't covered with cobwebs.

"It needs a lot of work," admitted Floria. "But the design is classic and has heaps of potential."

The traditional flagstone flooring was chipped and cracked, and a team of contractors were pulling it up piece by piece and taking the tiles outside into the garden.

"Excuse the mess," called a lyrical voice from down the hall, and Mimi appeared. "They're gutting the interior before we can restore it."

"What a gorgeous place." Daisy embraced Floria's half-sister, who'd just arrived from Sydney. "I had no idea it was so spacious inside."

"Five bedrooms," Mimi told her, hugging her back. "But we're going to convert it into four, two with adjoining bathrooms." Daisy hadn't seen Mimi since her mother, the great opera diva Dame Serena Levanté, had passed away several years ago. Since then, Mimi had been busy making a name for herself in the music industry in her native Australia.

"How are you?" Daisy asked.

"I'm good." Mimi gave her a wide smile. She had a lovely heart-shaped face with the kind of flawless, glowing complexion that only celebrities seem to pull off. Her eyes were a striking green—identical to her late mother's—and she sported a crop of glossy, black hair cut in a fashionable style. A tiny diamante stud glittered in her nose. "A bit nervous about the upcoming European tour, but apart from that, everything's great."

"I'm sure they'll love you," Daisy said reassuringly. "Your latest single, 'That Night,' was a huge hit in the UK earlier this year. They didn't stop playing it on the radio." There was a rumor that Mimi had written it the night she'd met her husband, Rob.

Mimi grimaced. "I still feel like a small fish in a really big pond. Come on, let's sit in the kitchen, it's the only place that hasn't been dismantled yet. I'm afraid there's no heating, the boiler isn't working." She rolled her eyes. "Yet another thing that needs fixing."

"At least we can have a hot drink." Floria set about making tea. "You don't need to be nervous, Mimi. Didn't your manager say that your first gig at the O2 Arena has already sold out?"

"That's so exciting!" Daisy couldn't be happier for Mimi. She was so talented and from what Floria had told her, had worked extremely hard to get where she was. After her mother had died, leaving her and her sisters a substantial inheritance, she'd reinvented herself. She'd hired a voice coach, taken dance lessons, and hired a producer to record her demo tape. According to Floria, she'd put her heart and soul into her career, and amassed a legion of young fans in the process. After winning an ARIA, one of Australia's most prestigious music awards, she was broadening her horizons and exploring the international pop market.

Mimi crossed her fingers. "Let's hope the rest of Europe sells as well."

"When is your first concert date?" Daisy took a seat at the rustic wooden table. The kitchen was in slightly better shape than the rest of the house, but the units were old and out of date, and linoleum tiles had been laid over what Daisy suspected was a continuation of the period flagstone flooring. The whole place was crying out for a makeover.

"The fifteenth of January," Mimi told her, accepting a cup of tea from Floria and straddling a chair opposite Daisy. "You must come. I'll get you complimentary tickets."

"That would be amazing." Daisy grinned at Floria in excitement. "Thank you."

Mimi ran a hand through her hair. "I've taken a month off to get settled, although these renovations are a pain. I'm beginning to regret buying a house that required so much work."

"Holly Lodge desperately needed someone to take care of it." Daisy glanced at the paint peeling off the walls. "It's been empty for so long, and it's such a beautiful old place. You've really done the house, and the village, a favor by taking it on."

"The grounds are lovely too," added Floria, sitting down. "The garden extends into the meadows and beyond that, into Hinchley Wood, and there's a stream behind the cottage with the cutest cobblestone bridge over it."

"That bridge is falling apart." Mimi widened her eyes in warning. "Don't use it until it's been repaired. The landscapers are coming next week, but trying to find people to work over the holidays is like wishing for a Christmas miracle. I'm having to pay them a fortune."

"It's a pity you didn't get this done before you arrived," said Daisy. "You're not living here while this is going on, are you?"

"Oh, gosh no. I'm staying at Brompton Court with Floria and Josh." She patted her sister's hand. "They're putting me up."

"We've moved in for the holidays," added Floria, who had a townhouse in London's Chelsea district. She'd inherited Brompton Court, a grand country mansion, from her mother but didn't live there. Instead, it was run by the capable Violeta and her husband Pepe, the groundsman.

"Is Rob joining you for Christmas?" Daisy asked.

Mimi smiled at the mention of her husband. "Yeah, he's flying into Heathrow a few days before Christmas. Unfortunately, he has to stay and tie up some loose ends before he can knock off for the holidays." Rob Fallon was the owner of the Fallon Hotel Group, which boasted a collection of upmarket boutique hotels in most of the world's capitals, London included. But like Mimi, his base was in Sydney, Australia.

"At least he'll be here for Christmas," Daisy said.

"What about you, Daisy?" Mimi leaned forward over the back of the chair. Daisy noticed her nails were painted a shimmering green. "How are things at the salon?"

"Busy." She pulled a face. "It's a crazy time of year. We have back-to-back appointments and the staff are run off their feet. The nail bar, a new addition for us, is doing extremely well too."

"Well, it's nice of you to take time out to come and see me. We're all so grateful to you for solving Mother's murder. How is that handsome detective you were seeing?"

"Oh, I wasn't seeing him." Heat stole into Daisy's cheeks. "I was helping him."

"They're still not really seeing each other," chuckled Floria. "Even though Daisy's working with the police now in an official capacity."

"Really? What are you doing?" Mimi asked.

"I'm just helping them with a bit of profiling. It's a part-time thing."

"Don't be so modest, Dais," Floria interrupted. "She's a qualified criminal profiler now."

"Impressive." Mimi arched an eyebrow. "Pity about that detective, though. I was sure he fancied you."

A loud crash in the living room made them jump.

Daisy breathed a sigh of relief. *She* didn't know what her relationship with Detective Chief Inspector McGuinness was, so how could she explain it to anyone else?

"What was that?" Mimi leaped off her chair.

Daisy and Floria followed her into the lounge, where two red-faced contractors stood gazing at a sooty fireplace that was big enough to park a car in.

"What happened?" Mimi waved her hand in front of her face. A fine black mist hung in the air and a heap of blackened debris had fallen down the chimney.

"The chimney is blocked," one of the men told her. "Someone has wedged several wooden slats up it. We're trying to unblock it now."

"Wooden slats?" Floria frowned. "Why would they do that?"

"Maybe they didn't use it and wanted to shut off the draft?" Daisy suggested. These mammoth chimneys were often drafty. The one in her little cottage, which was a fraction of the size of Holly Lodge, had been the same until she had wood-burning ovens installed.

"Could be," agreed the other contractor. "We'll get it cleared and working properly, don't you worry."

"It'll look lovely once it's done," said Floria. "A real focal point."

"Why don't you show me the rest of the property?" Daisy gazed out of the windows at the expanse of garden and in the distance, the unspoiled meadows and the shadowy, purple wood. "I haven't been here since I was a kid. Back then it was owned by the Lyle family."

"They went bankrupt, apparently," said Mimi. "The real estate agent told me it's been empty since old Mr. Lyle passed away five years ago."

"So sad . . ." Daisy murmured. She had fond memories of picnicking in the meadows with her friends when she was a teenager, and later walking through the woods with Tim. She blinked. Now where had that come from? She hadn't thought about her ex-boyfriend in ages. Shaking her head, she followed Mimi and Floria outside, through patio doors that were so cracked and dirty it was impossible to see through them.

"These will have to be replaced," remarked Floria, echoing Daisy's thoughts.

"My interior designer, Tamara, is working with the building contractors. She did the Rochester, Rob's hotel in Mayfair, so I'm trusting her with Holly Lodge. She's got a wonderful eye for detail."

"I catered a fiftieth at the Rochester last month." Floria's company, Prima Donna Productions, organized events and parties for the rich and famous. "It's stunning. Tamara knows her stuff. You're in good hands."

"Wow, I can see how the lodge got its name. There's holly everywhere." Daisy ran her fingers over the distinctive jagged leaves on an oversized bush bursting with red berries outside the patio door. "It looks so Christmassy."

"Some of it will have to be cut back." Mimi stood in the middle of the garden and inspected the house. "It seems to have taken over."

From this angle, Daisy could see the window frames were cracked and peeling and many of the tiles on the roof were missing. It was a big job, expensive too. No wonder the old lodge had remained unoccupied for so long.

A gurgling stream ran through the bottom of the garden, and Floria was right: The curved cobblestone bridge looked like something out of a fairy tale. She could imagine a big, ugly troll hiding underneath amongst the bulrushes. "Once the garden is done, you can sit out here and listen to the babbling brook while you compose your songs," she mused.

Mimi gazed into the distance. "That's the idea. As soon as I saw the stream, I fell in love with the place. And the view stretches for miles over the meadows and into the woods. It's idyllic, and so different from my place in Sydney."

"Your property over there is stunning," said Floria, who'd been over to visit. "It's so modern and spacious, and you have a breathtaking view of the harbor bridge."

"Yes, but it's not green and lush like this." Mimi ran her hand along the top of the low stone wall that separated the stream from the garden and took a deep breath. "I love the smell of fresh country air."

"That's probably manure from the neighboring paddock," Floria pointed out.

Daisy laughed.

A guttural yell made them glance back at the house.

"I hope those guys aren't destroying that fireplace," muttered Mimi. "Tamara wants to preserve as many of the original features as possible."

"We'd better go and see." Floria set off up the garden path toward the lodge.

"I think you'll be very happy here," Daisy told Mimi as they followed her.

"I hope so. This will be our London base, so to speak, so we want to make it as homely as possible."

An eerie silence greeted them when they stepped through the open patio door into the living room. The two burly men were staring at the fireplace, their faces pale beneath the soot. A handful of other contractors had accumulated around them. All eyes were focused on the chimney.

"Is there a problem?" Mimi asked, then Floria gasped and grabbed her sister's arm.

"Mimi, look!"

Daisy took a step closer and her heart leaped into her throat. "Is—is that a body?"

Through the black dust, she saw the figure of a man lying in a crumpled heap on the charred bricks. He was surrounded by broken boards and covered in dirt and grime.

"He toppled out of the chimney when we took out the last of the boards," said one of the contractors. "Goodness knows how long he's been up there."

"Oh, Lord." Mimi's hand flew to her mouth.

Daisy bent down to have a closer look.

"Careful, Daisy," urged Floria, who was still clutching her sister's arm.

Daisy waved away the dust and stared down at the unfortunate man. His skin was sallow and tight across his face like parchment stretched to breaking point. His vacuous eyes were sunken into his head, exposing the sockets. Thin strands of gray hair protruded from his leathery scalp like a zombie version of Einstein. It was then she saw the dark, gaping wound at the side of his head covered in congealed blood. She studied it for some time, before her eyes were drawn away by his beard. Despite the thinning hair and obvious decomposition, he had a full, white fluffy beard. It couldn't possibly be real. Then, she noticed what he was wearing, and her eyes widened.

"Who is it?" whispered Floria. "Do we know him?"

"I'm afraid so." Daisy turned to face them. "It's Father Christmas—and he's been murdered."

Chapter 2

"Is that who I think it is?" Detective Chief Inspector Paul McGuinness from the Surrey Criminal Investigation Department stared at the crumpled body lying in a sooty heap at the base of the fireplace.

"I'm afraid so," muttered Daisy, who'd called him before the dust had settled around the body. "Heaven knows how long he's been up there."

"Some time, I'd say," replied the forensic pathologist, Dr. Baker, who McGuinness had called en route. He was a middle-aged man with a receding hairline and a penchant for cryptic crosswords. Daisy knew this because his wife, Margaret, was one of her long-standing customers. Another white-clad crime scene officer was meticulously inspecting the inside of the chimney where the victim had been hidden.

"This house has been empty for almost seven years," Floria remarked over her shoulder. She'd recovered some of her color and was now giving DS Buckley, McGuinness's stoic sidekick, a statement.

"I don't think it's been as long as that." Baker extracted a hair sample with a pair of tweezers and carefully placed it into a plastic tube. "Possibly two years judging by the state of decay, but I'll know more once I've done the postmortem. The tight space and the lack of air in the chimney would have preserved the body somewhat."

Mimi wrinkled her nose. "How awful to think that he was up there the whole time when I was viewing the place and planning the renovations."

"At least he's been found now." Daisy put a reassuring hand on her arm. "And DCI McGuinness will find out who did this, won't you, Detective?"

The gruff detective glanced at her. Was it her imagination or did his chest puff out a tiny bit? "I'll certainly do my best. Who sold you the property, Miss Turner?"

Mimi glanced up at the use of her maiden name and the name she still used for her music. "It's technically Mrs. Fallon now. I got married in the summer."

McGuinness inclined his head. "Congratulations." He knew all three of Floria's half-sisters, having met them two years ago when their mother, Dame Serena Levanté, was murdered. He'd been the lead detective assigned to the case.

She managed a weak smile. "Thanks. To answer your question, it was Village Realtors in the High Street. The agent was a man called Cliff. No, sorry, Clive."

McGuinness gestured to Buckley, who scribbled hastily in his pad.

"Do we know who the victim is?" The detective studied the grubby corpse.

"There isn't any ID on the body," Baker confirmed. "Only this wedding ring on his left hand." He held up a transparent plastic evidence bag.

McGuinness peered at it, then shook his head. "No defining marks?"

"No, but I'll send it to the lab. We might be able to get a print or some DNA off it."

Daisy shook her head. "I don't recognize him, and I've lived in Edgemead most of my life."

"I don't know how you could recognize anyone looking like that," said Mimi. The stretched skin, the empty eye sockets, and the scraggly hair meant that the man had almost no identifiable features. He wasn't wearing a wristwatch, and there was no clue to his identity other than the Santa suit.

"We should be able to ID him through his dental records," supplied the pathologist helpfully. "He's still got most of his teeth. I'd say he was in his late thirties when he died."

"So young," mused Floria.

"If he had a wedding band, someone must have missed him," mused Daisy. How terrible to not know what happened to your husband. Distant memories of waiting for her ex-boyfriend, Tim, to get home and of him never materializing snuck into her brain. The worry caused by not knowing what had happened to him was something she'd never forget. Wrapping her arms around herself, she suppressed a shiver.

"We'll get on to missing persons." The detective glanced at Buckley.

"His poor wife," murmured Floria.

"Tell me again how you found him?" McGuinness asked the foreman who was hovering nearby. After the body had been discovered, Daisy had made him a cup of tea in the kitchen. The rest of the workers had been given the afternoon off, since they were being paid by the hour.

"We were clearing the chimney when we noticed those boards wedged across it." He gestured to the pile of broken wooden planks on the ground around the victim. "There were several of them positioned in such a way that they prevented the body from falling down." He pursed his lips. "When we removed them, that poor fella fell out. Didn't half give us a fright."

McGuinness thanked him, then turned to Buckley. "If you've taken his statement, he can go." Buckley led the relieved foreman away.

"My missus is never going to believe this," they heard him say, before Buckley showed him out.

McGuinness turned his attention to Daisy. "You must be a magnet for dead bodies. This is the third crime scene I've seen you at in as many years."

"It's not the only time you've seen me," she said softly, causing Buckley's brow to shoot up and McGuinness to redden.

He cleared his throat. "You know what I mean."

She spread her arms out in a gesture of defiance. "I came to Holly Lodge to visit Mimi. You can't blame this one on me."

"That's right," Floria said. "Daisy arrived an hour ago. Prior to that, I was here with Mimi and the construction team."

McGuinness turned to Mimi. "What made you decide to buy Holly Lodge?"

"My husband and I were looking for a UK base and

Floria suggested this old place. I loved it from the first moment I saw it—the faded grandeur, the classic interiors—it has so much potential. But to be honest, so far it's been one disaster after the next."

"This is just a glitch," Floria said, putting on a brave face. "Things can only improve from here on out."

There wasn't much that could beat a dead body falling out of the chimney, Daisy thought.

"What do you mean?" McGuinness frowned. "What other disasters?"

Mimi raked a hand through her short, spiky hair. "Oh, nothing. I'm just being melodramatic. Ignore me."

"I'd still like to hear." McGuinness studied her face and refused to look at Daisy. She knew he was still smarting over her loaded response. He took his professional reputation very seriously and wouldn't want his colleagues to know about his private life. Not that anything had happened between them. A few tentative dates, a lot of lingering looks, but so far, he hadn't so much as kissed her.

"Oh, it's this house," Mimi swept her arm around. "While I love it, it's been nothing but a headache. I know this isn't the best time of year to do renovations, but there have been countless delays and half the workforce is on leave, and now this." She shook her head. "Why didn't we buy some new-build in town?"

"You would hate it in town," stated Floria. "There's far too much traffic and not enough solitude. You did say you wanted peace and quiet in which to work. This is a majestic old place and once it's done up, it'll be magnificent. Holly Lodge deserves a second chance and you're the perfect person to give it a new lease on life."

Daisy agreed. "Think of what it'll be like once it's

complete. You'll be able to sit outside on the veranda and admire the view while you compose your next hit single."

"And have us over for summer barbeques." Floria grinned.

Mimi scrubbed at her eyes. "Yes, you're right. I'm still jet-lagged and seeing this dead body was the final straw."

"You can go, if you like." McGuinness's face softened a little. "I know where to find you if I need you." Brompton Court, the family's country mansion, had been the scene of Floria's mother's murder, and like all his crime scenes, he knew it intimately.

"That's probably a good idea," agreed Daisy. "You don't have to be here. Forensics will take some time to process the scene and you can't do any more work on it today. Why not go to Brompton Court and relax and make a fresh start tomorrow?"

"It might be longer than that before you can start working on the house again," warned McGuinness. "It depends how long it takes to gather all the evidence. I wouldn't schedule anything until after Christmas."

"Oh, dear." Mimi wrung her hands together. "We've still got so much to do."

"We'll be in touch," McGuinness said matter-of-factly. Daisy knew he couldn't make any promises. These things took time.

She walked them out. After hugging her, Floria said, "Daisy, you will help us figure out who did this, won't you?"

Daisy hesitated. "I'd like to, Flo, but you know DCI McGuinness. After the last time . . ."

Floria scoffed. "That was ridiculous. You should never have been arrested in the first place. He should have known you wouldn't kill anyone, let alone one of your own customers."

Daisy shrugged. "He was just following the trail of evidence and unfortunately, it did all point to me." She didn't like to think about how close she'd come to spending the next twenty years behind bars.

"Whatever." Floria waved her remark away as if it was too ridiculous a notion to dwell on. "I still want you to help us find out who this guy is. We need to clear this up as soon as possible and put it behind us. Mimi has enough on her plate with the renovations and her debut British tour coming up. She doesn't need the extra stress."

"I know." Daisy glanced at Mimi, who was already in the car, her head leaning against the headrest. "I'll do my best."

Floria squeezed her hand. "I know you will."

"It's the head wound that killed him," Dr. Baker was saying when Daisy walked back inside.

McGuinness frowned when he saw her. "What are you doing here? I thought you'd left with the others."

"Oh no, I was just seeing them off." She smiled sweetly at him. "I thought I'd come back to see if I could be of assistance."

He eyed her warily. "What assistance did you have in mind, Daisy? You've already said you didn't know the victim."

"No, but I know several hundred customers who may have known him," she replied. "Or at least heard about someone who went missing in a Santa suit two years ago. It's not every day a man dressed like that disappears into thin air."

McGuinness took a deep breath. "We'll identify him soon enough. You heard Dr. Baker. He's got nearly a full set of teeth. You don't need to do anything on your side."

Dr. Baker grunted in agreement.

"Still, don't you want to know what happened? Maybe one of my customers can shed some light? They might know his wife. Someone will have missed him."

The muscle in his jaw tensed as he studied her. She knew he was thinking how useful her local knowledge had been in previous cases. She'd provided him with valuable insights into the suspects and witnesses. Integrating himself with the local community was not one of McGuinness's strong points, and he knew it. He was better at staring his suspects down over the interrogation table or intimidating them into confessing.

Eventually, he relented. "Okay, but don't go spreading it around like wildfire. Let's wait until we know who this guy is before we start asking questions."

Daisy perked up. "You're saying I can help you?"

"Unofficially, Daisy. Please be careful. Don't forget the person who did this is still out there."

That gave her pause. Dr. Baker was bagging the dirty, white beard.

"He'd have to be quite strong to wedge a fully-grown man up a chimney, don't you think?" She stared at the body, her head tilted to one side.

McGuinness's eyes narrowed. "Yes, I do think."

"I'd say it's most likely to be a man."

"Most likely, but a strong woman could have done it too, or perhaps more than one perpetrator. We have to keep an open mind at this point in the investigation."

"True." She hesitated. "Shall I profile the killer for you, based on what we know so far? I've finished my criminology degree. I'm qualified to work with the police now."

Dr. Baker glanced at McGuinness. "This new age stuff is beyond me. I follow the science, not these so-called experts' educated guesses."

Daisy knew McGuinness was of the same opinion. "Nothing beats good old detective work," was one of his favorite sayings. She was expecting him to turn her offer down, so she was surprised when he said, "Why not? If it makes you happy, go ahead."

She ignored his condescending remark. "Okay, great." This was a chance to put her qualification to good use. She was by no means an expert, so-called or otherwise, but she was going to give it her best shot. Criminal profiling, although popular in London and the other big cities, was not something that had filtered down to the sleepy villages of the home counties.

An ambulance arrived to take away the body, so McGuinness ushered Daisy out. The weak winter sun had slunk behind a monstrous gray cloud and it looked like rain. "I'll see you tomorrow, Daisy. Remember, not a word until we've figured out who our victim is."

"Yes, I heard you the first time," she said as he walked her to her car. "I'll wait to hear from you before I start asking around."

"Good." He waited until she was inside the vehicle, then closed the door for her. She raised a hand in good-bye, and reversed out of the driveway.

As Holly Lodge grew smaller in her rearview mirror, she shivered. DCI McGuinness's warning rang in her ears. There was still a killer out there and he or she would be none too pleased that their victim's body had been unearthed after all these years.

Chapter 3

"Excuse me," Daisy called as she squeezed through the throng of people outside her hair salon, Ooh La La, the next day. This crowd was worse than the Boxing Day sales at Harrods.

Penny, her senior stylist, opened the door and Daisy slipped into the calm, warm interior of her hairdressing parlor. "Thank goodness," she breathed in relief as the noise outside became a muted murmur and the relaxing cords of Tchaikovsky's *The Nutcracker* filled the air. "What on earth is going on?"

"It's the news of the body you found at Holly Lodge," Penny explained, ushering Daisy to the tiny kitchen at the back where the kettle was already bubbling away. "It was on the local news this morning and now everybody wants to know what happened."

So much for keeping it under wraps. How had the press got hold of the story? Someone must have leaked it. McGuinness would not be impressed. "Bad news travels fast."

"Especially in a small village like this one." Penny made her a coffee and added a liberal spoonful of sugar. At Daisy's raised eyebrow, she added, "You're going to need it."

"I've said it before and I'll say it again, murder is good for business." Krish, her flamboyant senior stylist and the salon's manager, sauntered into the kitchenette. He was flushed and excited. "Daisy, you have to tell us what happened. Quickly, before we open up."

The small back room wasn't really big enough for the three of them, so Daisy suggested they move into the salon where Asa, her nail technician, was setting up her workstation, and Bianca, the Polish assistant Daisy was training, was cleaning the basins, ready for the coming rush.

"There's nothing to tell, really," she began, earning herself some raised eyebrows. Her friends knew her too well. She raised a hand. "Okay, I went to visit Mimi, Floria's sister, who's just arrived from Australia. You know she's bought Holly Lodge?"

"I love that old place," Krish enthused. "The chandeliers are to die for."

"You mean the abandoned property out on the Cobham Road?" Penny cocked her head to one side. Her long red hair, tied back in a ponytail, swung over her shoulder. Penny was a part-time model and easily the most glamorous of all her friends, but she didn't flaunt it. Instead, she chose to work as a hairdresser and used modeling to supplement her income. Fortunately, she was in such de-

mand that she could afford to do that. Her alabaster color-
ing and flaming red hair made her an attractive prospect
for certain brands. "I'm a niche market," she was fond of
saying in her easy, self-deprecating manner.

"I can't believe Mimi's bought that old place." Asa,
the Afro-Caribbean nail technician, came over to join in
the conversation. She was drinking Diet Coke from the
bottle, her nails a Christmassy red with silver sparkles.
"It's so exciting having a celebrity in the neighborhood."

Asa and the rest of the gang had also met Mimi when
she was last in the country for her famous opera diva
mother's funeral two summers ago.

"But how did you find the body?" asked Penny, bringing them back on track.

"I didn't find it," Daisy clarified. "Floria, Mimi, and I
were walking in the garden when we heard this almighty
crash. We ran back inside to see what had happened, and
there he was, lying at the base of the chimney. He'd fallen
out when the workmen removed some old beams that
were lodged in there."

"Was he really dressed as Father Christmas?" asked
Asa.

"Yes, complete with white, fluffy beard. It was surreal.
Of course, I called DCI McGuinness straight away."

"Of course you did." Daisy ignored him.

"I'd be too scared to call 'im," muttered Asa before
taking an enormous glug of her Diet Coke. Earlier in the
year, before Daisy had been arrested, he'd interrogated
every member of her staff and Asa, who wasn't a fan of
the police, was now more intimidated by the serious,
hulking detective than ever.

"Do they know who the dead man is?" Penny asked.

"No, they haven't a clue. It looks like he may have

been there for some time. In fact, DCI McGuinness didn't want me to mention anything until they'd ID'd him."

"Yeah, right." Krish glanced at the gathering crowd outside the glass doors. It was five past nine. They'd have to let them in now.

"Are we ready?" Daisy finished her coffee and collected the cups, which she took to the kitchen. They all scuttled to their workstations, while Daisy took up her position behind the reception desk. She'd do her best to field most of the questions, but it looked like it was going to be a trying morning.

"Let's let those who have appointments in first," Daisy suggested to Krish, who was unlocking the front door.

"That would be Liz, Delia, and someone called Anne-Marie. She's a new customer."

"Okay, great." Daisy took a steadying breath. "Let's do this."

"Appointments only," yelled Krish over the noisy throng.

"Excuse me," called Liz Roberts, the formidable head of the Edgemead Women's Institute, elbowing her way to the front. "Stand back, please. I have a booking."

Krish let her in and Penny directed her to a plush, leather swivel chair in front of a gilded mirror where she collapsed. "Heavens, it's like match day at Twickenham Stadium out there."

"Sorry, Liz," apologized Daisy, offering her a weary smile. "Can I get you a cup of tea or something?"

"Water would be lovely," she replied. "Sparkling, if you have it."

Daisy got her a drink while Krish let a pink-cheeked Delia Andrews in. Delia, a big-boned, horsey-looking woman with a protruding upper lip and large teeth, was in charge of the Edgemead Equestrian Centre, and one of Daisy's more recent customers. She'd finally succumbed to her partner, Lauren's, advice and now had a weekly standing appointment to have her frizzy chestnut mane straightened. "It was hell to fit under a riding hat," she'd admitted to Daisy, the first time she'd come in.

"What is this I hear about a murder at Holly Lodge?" she asked the second she got inside. Delia wasn't one to beat around the bush.

"Daisy found a man in a Santa suit stuffed up the chimney," explained Krish, showing her to her chair. Daisy frowned at him. He really was the most irrepressible gossip and not always technically correct, either, but she supposed it was close enough.

"How awful." Delia blinked her brown eyes at him in the mirror. "Do they know who he is?"

"Haven't a clue." Krish untied her wild hair that immediately sprung out in all directions. "They're waiting on DNA evidence. Dental records, you know."

"I wonder if it's anyone we know," mused Delia.

"It's quite possible," said Liz, who knew an awful lot of people. She and her husband, a dog-food billionaire, were very well connected in the community.

"I don't recall anyone going missing, though." Liz crinkled her forehead.

"No, neither do I." Delia pursed her lips. The ex-Olympic rider had lived in Edgemead all her life and knew everyone in the horsey set. Niall Barclay, Penny's much older beau and a world-renowned horse breeder, was a personal friend.

Next to come in was a short, rotund woman with a

jolly smile and lovely, thick auburn hair. She wore a scarlet jumper with *All I Want For Christmas Is Yule* emblazoned across it. This must be Anne-Marie.

"I don't think we've met." Daisy greeted the woman. "I'm Daisy Thorne."

"Anne-Marie Williams." The woman held out her hand. "I just need a wash and blow-dry before I meet a prospective client this afternoon."

"We can definitely help you with that, Mrs. Williams," said Daisy, smiling.

"Please, call me Anne-Marie."

"Well, if you follow me, Anne-Marie, Bianca will wash your hair now." She led the woman to the basins at the back of the salon. As the customer sat down, Daisy couldn't help but notice the dazzling array of costume jewelry on her fingers.

"This is a beautiful salon. I love what you've done with the place."

"Thank you." Daisy glanced fondly around the inside of the salon. Ooh La La was her pride and joy and she'd done most of the renovations herself after she'd bought it almost a decade ago.

"I work for the National Trust," Anne-Marie said, puffing out her impressive chest. It was clear she was proud to work for Europe's largest historic conservation charity. "So I have an eye for period pieces. I do love how you've restored the traditional Victorian radiators and the reclaimed pine floorboards. It gives the place a really authentic feel."

Daisy beamed. She was beginning to like Anne-Marie. "Thank you, that means a lot."

Anne-Marie seemed to want to chat. Daisy glanced at the growing queue outside the door, but let her continue.

"I'm meeting Floria Graham, the late Dame Serena Levanté's daughter, at Brompton Court later today. She's thinking about selling the estate to the trust."

"Really?" This was news to Daisy. Floria hadn't mentioned anything about it, but that might be because she was so busy with her party-planning business, being a new wife to Josh, and with Mimi's arrival. They hadn't had a proper catch-up in weeks, something Daisy needed to rectify ASAP.

"Floria loves that house," said Krish, who'd overheard. His ears were like satellite dishes for picking up random bits of gossip. "She'd never sell it to the National Trust."

Daisy sent him a warning glance, but Anne-Marie wasn't fazed. "Oh, I know she's fond of the place, but like all these old country mansions, they're so expensive to keep, and often it makes more sense to let someone else look after them."

Daisy could understand that. Brompton Court was a twelve-bedroom country estate that stood empty most of the year now that Serena had passed away. Once it had been the center of her whirlwind opera-singing lifestyle, filled with guests and host to countless notoriously debauched parties, but now its glamorous history was just a fading memory. It was looked after by Serena's Italian housekeeper, Violeta, and her husband, the groundsman Pepe, but with just the two of them, it was falling into disrepair. Floria sometimes stayed there at the weekend with her husband, Josh, and now Mimi was living there until Holly Lodge was ready for occupation, whenever that might be, but other than that, the old place was deserted.

Daisy herself remembered attending several of Serena's famous garden parties in the years before the opera diva's untimely death. They were always dazzling affairs with elaborate marquees, classical orchestras, and Europe's most famous musicians and composers in attendance.

"It would be good to see it restored to its former glory," she admitted, shrugging off the pang of nostalgia.

"That's what I thought," said Anne-Marie. "Our natural heritage should be enjoyed by everyone, and not just the elite few."

Daisy changed the subject. "Well, I'll leave you in Bianca's capable hands. Once you're done, come and take a seat at one of the workstations."

The petite Polish girl helped Anne-Marie get comfortable and Daisy rushed across the salon to open the front doors. "Come on in," she said to the excited crowd. There were at least twenty people waiting outside. She knew some of her regulars had come to gossip and didn't require an appointment, while others had come under the pretense of getting their hair done in order to find out what Daisy had discovered at Holly Lodge. Mimi Turner taking up residence in Edgemead was the most exciting thing to happen in the village since Dame Serena had been murdered.

There was a surge for the counter. Daisy greeted her regular customers by name, then began to take bookings. Before she knew it, her appointment book was full. "I'm sorry," she said to the remaining few. "I've got nothing else for today. How about tomorrow?" There were several nods of agreement, so Daisy turned the page and kept writing. Unsurprisingly, Krish was the most popular stylist, since everybody knew how he liked to gossip.

"Daisy, is it true Mimi Turner has bought Holly Lodge?" asked Beatrice, the baker's wife. Many of the customers with bookings had opted to wait in the comfy entrance and chat, rather than go outside into the cold. It was getting rather stuffy inside, so Daisy threw open the door and let the crisp air come in.

"Darling, it's a bit nippy," complained Liz, almost immediately. Daisy shut the door again.

"Yes, Mimi and her husband have bought Holly Lodge and are in the process of renovating it," she said.

"It's about time someone bought that old place," commented Liz, her hair in foils. "It's been empty since Mr. Lyle passed away. Poor man. I used to take his dog, Sago, for walks when I was younger. Extra pocket money, you know." She gazed dreamily at her reflection.

"Did you live close to the lodge?" asked Daisy.

"Oh, yes. My parents' house was just off Cobham Road."

Liz lived on the green in Edgemead in a large, triple-story Georgian townhouse with her husband, Roy, the dog-food billionaire. They were upstanding citizens, did a lot for local charities, and it was rumored that Liz was going to run for mayor in the not-too distant future.

"He was a funny old thing," crooned Mrs. Robbins, nudging Beatrice to make room for her walker. At ninety-three, she was Daisy's oldest customer. "He'd be turning in his grave if he knew that his grand old lodge had turned into a crime scene." She looked rather delighted by the prospect.

"Well, hopefully it won't be for long," Daisy set about combing through Anne-Marie's hair. "I know Mimi is anxious to get the building work finished."

"It's a big job," pointed out Krish. "That place is falling apart."

"Which place is this?" inquired Anne-Marie.

"Holly Lodge," Daisy told her. "It's a lovely Georgian house on the outskirts of Edgemead. I think at one point it was the hunting lodge for Cobham Manor. A friend of mine has recently bought it."

"I'd love to take a look." Anne-Marie's brows shot right up. "If that's okay with your friend? I'm fascinated by historical buildings."

"I can ask her," Daisy said. "I can't see that she'd have a problem with it."

"Excellent." Anne-Marie rubbed her hands together as the hair dryer went on.

The last customer left at 6:45 after a very long day. Daisy, Krish, Penny, and Asa were wearily tidying their workstations and cleaning the salon before they went home. Penny's train left at 6:53, so as soon as she was done, she grabbed her coat off the coat stand. "I've got to dash, guys. See you tomorrow."

She left, nearly colliding with a dark shape who'd pulled the door open. DCI McGuinness strode in, his coat billowing out behind him. Asa took one look at the somber detective, grabbed her jacket and backpack, and scampered out the back. Meanwhile, Krish eyed him approvingly. "Hello, Inspector. It's nice to see you again."

"Krish." McGuinness nodded a greeting.

"I'll be heading off then, Dais." Ooh La La's manager shot Daisy a knowing look. "See you tomorrow."

"Bye, Krish. Thanks for your help today."

"No problem. Have a good evening." And he waltzed out the door into the freezing night air.

"It looks like snow," McGuinness remarked, standing

in the middle of the salon. He seemed to make it smaller by just being there.

Daisy stopped what she was doing. "You're not the first person to say that to me today. It must be something in the air."

"The odds of a white Christmas are ten-to-one, if you listen to the bookies," he said.

"It would be lovely to have a white Christmas." She gestured to the vintage ball-and-claw sofa just inside the entrance. "Won't you sit down? Can I get you something to drink?"

He hesitated. "I don't want to put you out."

"Oh, don't worry about that. It's been a long day and I'm about to reward myself with a glass of wine. Will you join me?"

He hesitated, then shook his head. "I can't. I'm still on duty."

"Sparkling water then?"

He nodded.

"I'll be right back."

Daisy poured them each a glass—the wine could wait—and sat down opposite him on the matching velvet footstool. His long legs stretched out in front of him, almost touching hers. The entire interior of the salon was designed in a shabby-chic style, which was both glamorous and cozy at the same time. She loved the space and couldn't believe it had been almost ten years since she'd bought it. Where did the time go?

She glanced at McGuinness. There was only one reason why he'd visit her in person. "I take it you have some news regarding the identity of our mystery Santa?"

He grimaced. "It's hardly a mystery. Have you seen the papers this afternoon?"

Daisy shook her head. "Haven't had a chance." But she could guess. If the crowd outside her door this morning was anything to go by, it was all over the news.

"No, of course not. Well, someone leaked it and now the commissioner has ordered a department-wide inquiry into our media snitch." He sighed. "An internal investigation is the last thing we need."

Daisy waited for him to calm down. He took a sip of water, then said, "We've managed to identify our victim from the dental records. His name is Thomas Pierce and he disappeared on Christmas Eve two years ago."

Chapter 4

Daisy pondered the name. "Thomas Pierce? I don't think it rings any bells. Is he local?"

"No, but his wife lives in Esher. I'm going to pay her a visit this evening. She'll want to know her husband has been found after all this time."

Daisy sat up straighter. Esher wasn't far away, being the next town along the River Thames from Edgemead. "Can I come?"

He blinked at her. "You want to come with me to inform the next of kin?"

She nodded eagerly.

"It's not a particularly enjoyable job. The family is often distraught and it can be very distressing. I usually take a family liaison officer with me, but I understand that Pierce's wife has remarried, so I don't think that will be necessary."

"It will still be a shock," Daisy gave him a sideways glance. "Besides, aren't family liaison officers trained to look for evidence in case the next of kin might have had something to do with the crime?" She remembered learning that in her criminology course.

McGuinness looked put out. "I'm quite capable of doing that myself. Besides, our usual FLO is on leave and I don't think this is worth sending someone from another department."

"Do you suspect her?"

McGuinness shrugged. "The spouse is always the first person we look at in cases such as these."

Daisy knew that, and he had more than enough experience to be able to suss out whether the grieving widow's reaction was suspicious. "Does that mean you'll take me with you? I am cleared to work with the police now, as a consultant."

He gave a slight nod, but it was enough to make her heart surge. "Thank you, Paul. Oh, by the way, I've done a criminal profile of the killer."

"You have?" He eyed her suspiciously.

"Yes, I said I would." When he didn't react, she prompted. "Do you want to hear it?"

He leaned back on the sofa, his expression unreadable. "Sure, go ahead."

"Right, let me get my notes." She pulled out her phone and tapped until she got to the place where she'd written them down. "Okay, so I started with the location of the crime—Holly Lodge. Why there? Of course, it's isolated and surrounded by extensive grounds, so there'd be nobody around to hear or see them, but the killer must have known that, which means he was familiar with the place."

McGuinness eyed her cautiously. "Assuming it's a he."

"Well, the victim was a fully-grown male, at least eighty kilograms, and a deadweight at that, so the perpetrator would have to have considerable strength to shove him up the chimney and then board it up. Besides, statistically the murderer is more likely to be a man."

"Or there was more than one person," the detective added.

She held up her hands. "Okay, that is possible, but only one person hit him on the head."

McGuinness studied her. "That's true, and I agree, the killer must have been familiar with the area."

"Not necessarily." Daisy caught his eye. "I said familiar with the place, not the area. Maybe the killer had viewed the property and remembered it was empty. After all, it was on the market. He may not have known the area very well at all. In fact, he may not even have been from here."

McGuinness drummed his fingers on the side of his glass. "How do you get to that conclusion?"

She raised a finger. "All in good time."

He leaned back, waiting for her to continue.

Daisy glanced down at her notes. "I looked at the way the killer attempted to hide the body. He must have known that stashing it up the chimney was only a temporary solution and that it would be discovered eventually. The house was up for sale. He didn't know it wouldn't be sold for another two years."

McGuinness watched her silently.

"I'm thinking that maybe he wasn't from the area. He

just needed the body to be hidden for long enough to make a clean getaway."

"Hmm . . ." McGuinness scratched his chin, where a smattering of dark stubble was forming. "You may have a point there."

"It ties in with the property-hunting theory," she added. "Except, he decided not to stay in Edgemead after the murder."

"What about the Santa suit?" McGuinness asked.

"Well, that is strange. Obviously, the victim was on his way to a Christmas event or coming back from one when he was killed. He was playing the part of Santa, so maybe the event was something to do with kids, like a football club or a school function."

McGuinness pursed his lips. "But how did he end up at Holly Lodge?"

"That's the strange bit," confessed Daisy. "He must have got there somehow. Either he was lured there, in which case what happened to his car? Or he went with someone else, in which case he knew his killer."

McGuinness frowned. "I'll check to see if any cars were found abandoned at Holly Lodge around Christmastime two years ago. It may have been removed and impounded."

"That's a good idea. If not, he may have met his killer and they went there together. I can't think why he'd go en route to a function or on his way home, however, unless it was something urgent. Something that couldn't wait."

"We need to speak to the estate agent," McGuinness said.

"I'm not done." Daisy paused to take a sip of her water.

"Please, do go on." The corners of his mouth turned up.

"Then there's the murder weapon."

"We didn't find anything at the crime scene," McGuinness cut in. "We searched it thoroughly."

"No, but it was obviously a hard, blunt object, judging by the damage caused."

"The pathologist thought it was a hammer."

Daisy raised her eyebrows. "That helps with my profile. The killer must have taken the weapon with him to meet the victim, which means this was carefully planned. The location, the fact the victim was taken by surprise, the hammer blow—all indicates premeditation on the part of the killer."

"I agree," said McGuinness. "I bet I know what you're going to say next?"

Daisy gestured for him to go ahead. "Please . . ."

"You're going to say, What kind of man chooses a hammer as a murder weapon? A workman, maybe? A carpenter?"

"Exactly. It is possible he brought it with him, but it's more likely it was already in his truck or car. If I was going to kill someone, I'd probably take a knife, not a hammer. The fact that he thought to use a hammer is significant."

"You'd use a knife?" McGuinness arched his brow. "I'll bear that in mind."

"Hypothetically speaking," she added quickly. The stabbing he'd arrested her for earlier in the year was still fresh in her mind.

"So we're looking for a strong man who works in construction and was viewing property in the Edgemead area?"

She waved her hand in the air. "Possibly. Although, the

property-viewing theory is only that: a theory. A builder is unlikely to be able to afford a property like Holly Lodge, so if he wasn't viewing it as a prospective buyer—"

"He could have been working on it," finished McGuinness, straightening up.

"Was there work being done on the property two years ago?" Daisy said, thinking out loud. "Maybe the council was doing maintenance in the area or the trust that owned the house since Mr. Lyle's death were doing some renovations."

"It's worth looking into," McGuinness said. "I must admit, you've given me a few new leads to follow up."

Daisy couldn't resist a grin. "See, not just new-age mumbo jumbo. Anyway, I'm glad to be of service."

He studied her over his glass. "You, Daisy Thorne, are unlike any other woman I've ever met."

She flushed. "I'll take that as a compliment."

"You should." He chuckled, a rare occurrence. It was nice to see his eyes light up. He was very attractive when he smiled, a fact that was often lost beneath his permanent scowl and brooding demeanor.

"Did you find out anything today?" she asked. "Other than the victim's name?"

"Only what I've told you, that the murder weapon was a hammer. The postmortem was performed. There was no DNA found on the body; it was too badly decayed to hold any forensic evidence."

Daisy had expected as much. "None of my customers remembered a man disappearing in recent years," she said. "Which adds to my theory that he wasn't from here."

"Or your customers didn't know him," McGuinness

pointed out reasonably. "Not everyone in the village came into your shop today."

Daisy snorted. "It certainly felt like it. We had queues twenty people deep when we arrived this morning and it didn't let up during the day. Everybody wanted to know what happened at Holly Lodge."

McGuinness shook his head. "Some people have a macabre fascination for crime."

"It's because it's Mimi Turner's new house," Daisy explained. "A local celeb involved in a murder mystery . . . That makes it doubly newsworthy."

"How's Mimi taking it?" McGuinness asked.

Daisy grimaced. "As well as can be expected. She's pretty stressed right now. Floria is looking after her at Brompton Court, and her husband is arriving on Christmas Eve."

"That's good." McGuinness got to his feet. "Shall we get going? We've got a next of kin to visit and it's getting late."

Daisy glanced out of the window. It was already pitch-black outside, the sun having set hours ago. "Just let me lock up, and I'm all yours."

Hannah Collington lived in an affluent suburb of Esher, which was itself a rather upmarket town. As they turned off the well-lit High Street and into a road flanked by frosty meadows interspersed with freestanding modern houses, McGuinness said, "Hannah's new husband is the real estate agent who sold Holly Lodge to Mimi."

Daisy stared at him. He'd certainly kept that little

nugget to himself. "Really? Now that is interesting. He would have known about Holly Lodge."

"Yep. I'm also wondering when exactly Hannah met her new husband."

"You mean, was she seeing him before Thomas disappeared?"

He raised his eyebrows.

Daisy pondered this point as they drove past an idyllic village green complete with duck pond and an enormous weeping willow. The water was partly frozen and the shattered ice on the top resembled shards of glass glittering in the pale moonlight. If Hannah had met her new husband, the real estate agent, prior to Thomas's death, it would give them a motive. Motive and opportunity.

"Do you think they plotted Thomas's demise to get him out of the way?" she asked.

McGuinness glanced across at her. "That is what we have to find out."

The neat double-story semidetached house was situated one road back from the green. Like many of the other houses in the street, it was strung with fairy lights and a decorative candelabra stood in one of the upstairs windows. There was a short driveway out front where a black SUV was parked. The hefty vehicles were popular with young, wealthy mothers whose husbands could afford to pay for the additional security a 4x4 offered. Of course, they were far too wide for the narrow country lanes, not to mention how much fuel they guzzled.

McGuinness parked his BMW behind it and they got out. "Only one car?" Daisy remarked.

McGuinness rapped on the door, his features tense. A slender woman with tired eyes and hair in a messy bun opened it. "Hello?"

"Are you Hannah Collington?" McGuinness asked.

"Yes. Can I help you?" She had a soft, Scottish accent.

McGuinness flashed his ID card. "I'm DCI McGuinness from Guildford CID and this is Daisy Thorne. She's, er, she's working with the police. Can we come in?"

She wavered on the doorstep, then gave a reluctant nod and opened the door wider. It was then Daisy noticed she was heavily pregnant. They followed her into a messy living room with toys scattered over the carpet and the TV tuned to a kids' channel. "Excuse the mess. I've just put my daughter down for the night."

Daisy smiled to put her at ease. "How old is she?"

"Four." She gestured for them to sit down, hastily scooping up a fluffy pink bunny and a purple-haired troll off the couch. McGuinness eyed them warily.

"What is it you wanted to see me about, Detective?"

Daisy glanced around but couldn't see any evidence of Mr. Collington.

"Is your husband home?" McGuinness asked, echoing her thoughts.

"Oh, um . . . no. He's not back from work yet. He sometimes has late viewings."

McGuinness cleared his throat. "We've got some news about your first husband, Thomas Pierce."

Her eyes widened and she went a shade paler. Daisy saw her reach out and clutch the pink bunny. "What news? You haven't found him, have you?"

"Yes, we have."

She shut her eyes. "He's living with that tart, Lilly. Isn't he?"

Daisy frowned. "What tart?"

"That barmaid. The one he ran off with."

"Erm, no," McGuinness said, frowning. "I'm afraid

his body was found at a house near Cobham yesterday morning."

Mrs. Collington gawked at him. "You mean he's—he's dead?"

"I'm afraid so. I'm very sorry for your loss."

Hannah Collington didn't react. She just sat on the couch, hugging the stuffed toy over her round belly. "Hannah? Are you okay?" Daisy asked, as the silence stretched out.

Her voice was hollow. "All this time I thought he'd run out on me, but you're saying he was actually dead?"

Daisy's heart went out to her. "We're sorry to have to bring you such awful news."

"How did he die?" Her eyes were wild and unfocused.

"He was murdered," stated McGuinness.

Her hand flew to her mouth. "Murdered?"

"Yes, he'd been hit on the head." Daisy didn't mention the chimney or the Santa outfit. At least they could spare her that indignity.

"Do you know who did it?" she whispered.

"No, that's what we're trying to find out," McGuinness said. "Do you think you'd be able to help us by answering some questions?"

Her lip quivered. "I'll try."

Daisy stood up. "Why don't I make us some tea?"

Hannah waved a weak hand in the direction of the kitchen.

"Be gentle," Daisy mouthed to McGuinness. The sweet tea would help with the shock and maybe fortify Hannah enough so that she could talk about the events leading up to her husband's disappearance.

"Mrs. Collington, why did you think your husband had

run out on you and your daughter? I'm assuming she is Thomas's child?"

"Yes, Elly is Tom's. She was only two when Tom disappeared." She took a shaky breath. "I always suspected he was having an affair, and just before he went missing, I found out with whom."

"The barmaid?"

"Yes, that woman from the Coach and Horses. When I confronted her, she didn't bother to deny it."

Daisy listened from the adjoining kitchen. The interior of the house was open-plan and spacious, allowing their voices to travel. If Thomas had been having an affair, they now had another suspect. His mistress.

"Do you remember her name?" McGuinness asked. Daisy held her breath.

"How could I forget," snapped Hannah. Judging by her bitter tone, she hadn't got over the betrayal. "Her name was Lilly."

"You don't know her surname?"

"No. I didn't need to know any more than that."

"What did she say when you confronted her?" McGuinness wanted to know.

Hannah's shoulders stiffened. "At first she stared at me like I was mad, then she got all defensive and said she didn't want to speak to me. But I wasn't having any of that. I asked her straight out if she was sleeping with my husband. Everyone in the pub heard me."

"Did she admit to the affair?"

"She said they loved each other. Ha! Can you believe that? Tom was a sucker for a blonde in a short skirt. Trust me, I know. I told her she was wasting her time with him, and that he loved me and Elly and was just using her."

Her face crumpled. "Things had been tough between us for a while. I had postnatal depression after the baby was born. We weren't—" She stumbled over her words. "We weren't intimate."

"I'm sorry." Daisy returned with a cup of tea, which she handed to Hannah. "That must have been really hard." She hadn't made one for McGuinness or herself since they wouldn't be there long enough, and she knew from past experience that the detective didn't like imposing on suspects.

Hannah sniffed. "It was. Tom was preoccupied with building the business and I was left to cope by myself."

"Don't you have family nearby?" Daisy inquired. "Anyone to help you?"

"No, my parents live in Glasgow. Tom and I moved here after we got married." That explained the accent.

"Esher is a long way from Glasgow," commented McGuinness.

Hannah shrugged. "We wanted a fresh start and I'd been to Surrey on a school trip when I was younger and loved it, so I suggested moving here. We looked around for a town that was big enough to start a new business venture, but small enough to have a sense of community. That's why we settled on Esher."

"It's perfect for that," agreed Daisy.

Hannah gave her a tentative smile. "Yes, I love it here."

"What business venture did Thomas start?" asked McGuinness, glancing at Daisy.

"Oh, didn't I say? He started Village Realtors with Clive. Tom had been involved in property development in Scotland, so it made sense, but in order to afford the capital, he took on a partner. That's how I met my husband."

"Just to be clear, Clive, your current husband, was Thomas's business partner?"

"Yes, why is that so strange?" She gazed at them openly.

Daisy shook her head. "It's not strange, it's just a surprise, that's all. If you don't mind me asking, how did you marry again if you were still married to Thomas?"

Hannah's eyes hardened. "After Thomas disappeared, I applied for a divorce. At that point, I thought he'd run off with Lilly." Her voice wavered. "Obviously, I had no idea he was dead."

"Of course not," Daisy said.

"It wasn't the easiest process," Hannah continued. "I had to prove that I'd tried to find him but couldn't. Nobody knew where he was. Eventually, the court granted me a divorce in his absence."

"I see," McGuinness said.

Daisy leaned forward. "I'm sure Clive was a great help after Tom's disappearance."

Hannah took a sip of her tea and stared into the middle distance, remembering. "Yes, he was marvelous. I fell to pieces after Tom disappeared and he took care of me. Do you have any idea what it feels like to have the love of your life disappear one day and never come back?"

Daisy hesitated, then said quietly, "Actually, I do."

McGuinness glanced at her in surprise.

"A similar thing happened to me some years ago with an ex-boyfriend."

"Then you know what I was going through." Hannah reached forward and grabbed her hand like she was suddenly a kindred spirit, bonded by their mutual experience. "I was a mess. I was frantic with worry, but at the same time, filled with rage. I mean, how could he do something like that to us? Didn't he know we needed him?"

Daisy could relate to everything Hannah was saying. "Is that when you got together with Clive?" she asked gently.

Hannah released her hand. "Yes, Clive was amazing. I don't know what I would have done without him. He's a far better husband and father than Tom ever was, and Elly loves him to bits. I doubt she even remembers Tom. So when he proposed . . . of course, I said yes."

As if on cue, the amazing Clive walked through the door.

Chapter 5

"Honey, whose car is that in the drive? Oh, sorry, I didn't mean to interrupt." He scrutinized McGuinness before moving on to Daisy. She thought she glimpsed something unsettling in his gaze. Fear, maybe? But he pasted a smile on his face and held out his hand. "Hello, I'm Clive Collington and you are—?"

Hannah got to her feet, letting the bunny roll off her lap onto the floor. "Oh, honey, this is Detective Chief Inspector—?" She drew a blank. "Sorry, I've got baby brain."

"McGuinness from Guildford CID," he provided. "And this is my . . . er, this is Daisy Thorne, a consultant."

Daisy shot McGuinness a surprised glance. That was the first time he'd called her a consultant. She liked it; it had a good ring to it. Turning her attention back to Clive Collington, she shook his outstretched hand. His palm was like ice. He must have walked home, which meant the two of them shared the family car. Perhaps they weren't as well off as they'd have people believe. "Pleased to meet you, Mr. Collington."

Hannah went to her husband's side. "Can you believe they've found Tom?" She made it sound like he was a misplaced toy her daughter had lost down the back of the sofa.

Clive looked genuinely startled. "Found him? Where?"

"His body was discovered at an abandoned property near Cobham yesterday," McGuinness repeated. "In fact, it's one of your properties, Mr. Collington. Holly Lodge?"

Daisy watched Clive's reaction. He blinked several times as he digested McGuinness's words, then he gave a little shake of his head and frowned in confusion. If he was lying, he was pretty good at it. He seemed to have been thrown completely off-balance. "His body was found at Holly Lodge?"

"Here, why don't you sit down." Daisy vacated the sofa so the couple could sit next to each other and went to stand beside McGuinness.

"I don't understand." Clive sat and ran a hand through his hair. It was sprinkled with powder. It must have started snowing. "I sold Holly Lodge to Mimi Turner, the pop star, several months ago. How could his body be there?"

"The construction crew found it during the renovations," explained Daisy, keeping her voice even. "He died from a head wound."

Clive's eyes seemed to pop out of his head. "You mean someone killed him?"

Hannah clutched her husband's hand. "All this time he was dead, Clive. We thought he'd done a runner, but he was lying in that old house." She shivered, and he put an arm around her shoulders.

"I can't believe this. Are you sure it's him?"

"There's no doubt," confirmed McGuinness. "We've identified him through his dental records."

"Good lord." He dropped his head into his hands.

"Are you all right, Mr. Collington?" Daisy asked. Hannah rubbed her husband's back with one hand, the other rested on her belly. He appeared more upset than his wife had been on hearing the news.

"Yes." He glanced up. "It's just, I feel awful now. We all thought he'd run off with a barmaid from the local pub."

"Yes, Hannah told us," said Daisy. "You wouldn't happen to know her surname, would you?"

He scrunched up his eyes. "I think it was Rosewood. Lilly Rosewood. She disappeared the same time as he did, so everyone assumed they'd run off together. It was a known fact that they were having an affair." His voice was bitter, like he was personally affronted by their betrayal.

"She also disappeared?" McGuinness's head snapped up.

Hannah spoke up. "Yes, at the same time. That's why we assumed they'd gone off together."

McGuinness met Daisy's eye and she knew what he was thinking. If Thomas Pierce had turned up dead, who was to say Lilly Rosewood hadn't also been murdered? Maybe her body was also hidden at Holly Lodge?

McGuinness studied them thoughtfully, then he said, "Do you remember where you both were the evening Thomas went missing?"

"Now just a minute," blurted out Clive. "You're not insinuating we had anything to do with his death, are you?"

"It's routine questioning, Mr. Collington." Daisy gave him a reassuring smile. "Once we know where you were, DCI McGuinness can rule you out of the inquiry."

"Ah, I see." His shoulders relaxed.

McGuinness shot her a grateful look.

Hannah leaned back on the sofa. "I was at home with Elly. It was Christmas Eve. Tom was going to some charity event, but Elly hadn't been feeling well, so I didn't go. He was wearing this ridiculous Santa suit, but it was for a good cause. He was going to hand out presents to the kids."

That explained the costume.

"I could never understand why he left me wearing that," murmured Hannah, staring into the past. "I just assumed he kept other clothes at *her* house."

"Yeah, it was like he just walked out one night and never came back," added Clive. "He didn't take anything with him."

"Didn't that strike you as odd?" asked McGuinness.

"Of course it did, but we just thought he didn't want anything to do with his old life. We had no idea . . ." Clive petered off.

"Things hadn't been right between us for a while," Hannah reminded them, still holding her husband's hand. "So when he didn't come back, I thought he'd decided to leave me."

"When you say things hadn't been right between you,

what exactly do you mean?" McGuinness asked. "Was there something else other than your post-partum depression?"

Hannah hesitated, then she said, "Elly's birth had been hard and it took me a while to recover. We—we grew apart. He started going out more, mostly down to the local pub. That's where he met Lilly. I suppose he wanted what he couldn't get at home." She flushed, embarrassed by her admittance.

Clive patted her hand. "There was no excuse for what he did. He should have been there for you and the baby."

Daisy didn't disagree. Was Thomas Pierce the kind of man that bailed at the first sign of trouble?

"Where were you, Mr. Collington?" McGuinness fastened his steely-eyed glare on the real estate agent. Daisy felt the temperature in the room drop a few notches.

"I was at my parents' place in Yorkshire." He didn't meet McGuinness's gaze, but then, it was rather disarming. Daisy had been on the receiving end of that stare herself and knew what it felt like. She didn't envy Clive Collington one bit.

"Yorkshire?" McGuinness kept staring.

"Yes, I spent Christmas with them. I was there when Hannah rang me on Christmas Day to say Tom hadn't come home after the party. At first, I thought he'd made a night of it with the barmaid and would be home soon, tail between his legs, but when he didn't return, we started to worry."

Hannah rubbed her belly in small, clockwise motions. "That's right. I was distraught. Clive rang me on Boxing Day and Tom still wasn't home. In the end, I went to the pub to look for him, but they hadn't seen Lilly since the day before Christmas Eve. She'd missed her shift."

"Did you go to her house?" asked Daisy.

She looked sulky. "No, I didn't know where she lived and the bar manager wouldn't give me that information."

Daisy wasn't sure Hannah was telling the truth. If a woman suspected her husband was having an affair, surely she'd follow him to his lover's house to get proof, otherwise how would she know for sure?

"When did you get back from Yorkshire?" McGuinness wanted to know.

Clive scratched his head. "I got back on the evening of the twenty-sixth. I opened the agency on the twenty-seventh as we had several viewings lined up."

"Right, and I take it your parents will be able to confirm this?"

"Well, they would, except my father passed away some time ago and my mother is in a care home. Her mental faculties aren't what they used to be, but she may remember something." It didn't sound good. Daisy didn't hold out much hope. Even so, she knew McGuinness would check. He wasn't the type to leave any stone unturned.

"Thank you, Mr. and Mrs. Collington," he said, getting to his feet. "Once again, I'm sorry for your loss. We'll be in touch if we need anything else."

Hannah remained seated. It was Clive who showed them to the door. "I hope you don't think we had anything to do with Tom's murder," he said quietly. "My wife is in a very fragile state right now, and I don't want her unduly upset. This will obviously have come as a shock."

"We're keeping an open mind at this stage," McGuinness said noncommittally.

*   *   *

"What do you make of that?" Daisy asked, once they were back in the car and heading toward Edgemead. It was snowing quite heavily and the BMW's windshield wipers whipped back and forth in an unsuccessful attempt to clear it. Visibility was bad and made worse by the cloud cover that had swept in and blocked out the moon. McGuiness decreased his speed.

"I thought she looked genuinely shocked by the news of her husband's body being discovered." He kept his eyes locked on the road.

"So did Clive," Daisy added. "Although, he could have been faking it."

"His alibi will be hard to prove," McGuinness muttered. "Unless his mother can remember back to two Christmases ago."

"Unlikely," said Daisy. "Still, it's worth checking. She might not be as bad as he made out."

"I'll send Buckley." He slowed to a halt behind a truck that wasn't moving. There were several cars backed up in front of it, their brake lights glowing red through the driving snow. None of them were going anywhere. "Something's happened up ahead."

"It looks like a traffic jam." Daisy craned her neck to see around the truck. "It's backed up for miles. There must have been an accident."

"Bloody hell." He leaned back in his seat. "We have to find that barmaid, Lilly Rosewood. She may have been the last person to see Thomas Pierce alive."

Daisy gazed across at him. "You do realize she may also be dead."

"We don't know that yet. Let's not jump to conclusions." The traffic eased forward a few meters, then came to another halt.

"If they were going to run off together and we found his body, it stands to reason . . ." She left the sentence hanging.

"No, it doesn't. This isn't guesswork, Daisy, it's police work. We follow the train of evidence. She may be perfectly well and living in the south of France, for all we know."

"Odd that she disappeared at the same time as Thomas, then." Daisy shot him a look. "It's more likely she's also dead." She paused as the traffic inched forward. "Or she's the one who killed him."

Chapter 6

The snow pattered against the roof of McGuinness's BMW as they crawled toward Edgemead. There had indeed been an accident, a fact verified by the cavalcade of flashing blue lights that flew past them on the opposite side of the road a short time later.

"It looks like we might be here a while." Daisy sighed. At least it was warm inside the car and they had plenty of fuel, so there was no danger of being stranded. The radio was playing "I Saw Mommy Kissing Santa Claus" softly in the background. The car smelled faintly of his after-shave.

"Can I ask you a personal question?" he asked quietly.

Daisy's gut crunched into a hard ball. She'd expected this. "Um, sure."

"What did you mean when you said something similar happened with you and an ex-boyfriend?"

Daisy reddened. "Oh, that. It's nothing. I was just trying to empathize with Hannah. Get her to open up."

He turned to face her. "You might as well tell me, Daisy. We're not going anywhere fast. Did your boyfriend disappear?"

Daisy sighed. Why had she opened her big mouth? "Yes, but unlike in Hannah's case, he wasn't dead. He really did just leave me."

"I'm sorry," he murmured. "That must have been hard."

He had no idea how hard.

I saw Mommy tickle Santa Claus underneath his beard so snowy white, sang the radio.

"It happens." She tried to sound nonchalant but failed miserably. "Relationships end all the time. It's no big deal."

He raised an eyebrow. "When was this?"

She stared out at the falling snow. Illuminated by the car's powerful headlights, it looked like a multitude of tiny white spears being shot down from above. "A long time ago."

Was four years a long time? It didn't feel like it, but then so much had happened since then. She glanced across at McGuinness, only to find he was watching her intently, but his normally hard, steely gaze was softer and more silvery in the dim interior of the car. She may as well tell him what happened and get it over with, then they could move on to a more pertinent topic, like the investigation. There was still so much she wanted to discuss with him.

"I got home after work one day and Tim wasn't there.

He'd packed his things and gone. At first, like Hannah, I was frantic with worry. I was convinced something had happened because I refused to believe he'd walk out on me. We'd been living together for almost ten months by that stage and we were happy. At least, *I* thought we were." Memories of walking hand in hand along the river path and kissing beneath the weeping willow floated through her mind. "His leaving didn't make any sense. We hadn't even had a fight."

McGuinness frowned. "That does sound odd. Are you sure something didn't happen to him?"

"I'm sure. He'd taken all his belongings with him."

"But if you hadn't had a disagreement, there'd be no reason for him to leave." He'd switched to detective mode. His senses had been alerted to a possible mystery, except he was wasting his time. There was no mystery. "Maybe there was something going on that you didn't know ab–"

"He left a note," she interjected.

"Ah." McGuinness fell silent.

Daisy gnawed on her lower lip, recalling the icy tentacles that had clutched at her heart when she'd first read it. The pain had dulled over time, but the memory would forever be ingrained in her mind. She'd fallen to the floor, shaking like a leaf, unable to comprehend the words scrawled in Tim's handwriting in front of her. "He wrote that he was sorry, but he had to go. That was it."

"He didn't give an explanation?"

"No."

"And you didn't try to find him?"

Daisy flopped her head back onto the headrest. "Why? He left on his own accord. What was the point in looking for him?" It still hurt, even though she'd gotten over it years ago. The devastating realization that he wasn't coming back, followed by the humiliation of having to explain his sudden absence to her friends and acquaintances. If she was honest with herself, it was the humiliation that had been the hardest to bear. Her pride had been badly damaged, so much so that she hadn't had a serious relationship since. "There was no point."

There was a pause. Only the voice of the Jackson 5 could be heard saying what a laugh it would be if Daddy had seen Mommy kissing Santa Claus last night.

"I must say, I'm surprised at you." McGuinness broke the silence.

"What do you mean?" She glanced across at him, frowning, then relaxed when she saw his expression was kind, not judgmental.

"I know you, Daisy. You've got an inquisitive mind and an insatiable curiosity. I can't believe you didn't investigate Tim's disappearance, to find out why he left."

"I told you, there was nothing to investigate," she retorted, her voice curt. "He wanted out, he made that quite clear in his note. There was nothing suspicious about it. I wasn't going to go crawling after him."

McGuinness contemplated this. "You're right, it is best to move on in those situations."

"Exactly, there was no point in dragging it out. Besides, it was a long time ago. I barely remember him." She fidgeted in her seat. It was suddenly too warm in the car and the upbeat Christmas music was annoying her. She opened her window a smidgen and the icy air thrust through, cooling her hot cheeks.

"How long do you think we'll be stuck here?" she asked.

"Not long." He activated the siren, making Daisy

jump, then he eased the BMW out of the traffic jam onto the empty dual highway and drove slowly toward the flashing lights.

As they got closer, they could see what had happened. A vehicle had skidded across the icy intersection and collided with another car traveling in the opposite direction. Glass had scattered all over the road and there was a nasty dent in the front of one of the vehicles. A woman with minor injuries was being helped into an ambulance, while a man stood in the snow talking to the traffic police. McGuinness pulled up beside them and lowered his window.

"DCI McGuinness." He flashed his ID card. "What's the situation here?"

The officer pointed to the crash site. "The lady hit some black ice and skidded into the gentleman coming the other way."

"Any injuries?"

"No, sir. No one was seriously hurt."

McGuinness surveyed the scene. A tow truck had arrived and was reversing toward the woman's damaged vehicle. The man's car was still running, evident by the dimmed headlights and the mist cloud emanating from the exhaust. "That's good. Do you need my help with anything?"

The officer shook his head. "No, you're okay, sir. Thanks for stopping."

"Great. Mind if I pass? I'm escorting a witness home."

"Sure thing, sir."

The officer moved a barrier and waved McGuinness through. He carved around the two damaged vehicles and the tow truck, then veered back onto the left-hand side of the road.

Daisy narrowed her eyes at him. "And here I thought we were going nowhere fast."

His mouth turned up at the sides. "Perks of the job."

She didn't miss the glint in his eye.

"Thanks for letting me tag along," she said when he dropped her off outside her cottage. "It was an interesting evening." They'd said very little the rest of the way home. McGuinness had been concentrating on the road and Daisy was still smarting over how cleverly he'd manipulated her into talking to him about Tim. It seemed the handsome detective's skills weren't limited to the interrogation room.

As she climbed out of the car, the automatic security light over her front door went on, illuminating the front of the house and the short driveway where her trusty Honda was parked. She'd had the light installed earlier in the year after she'd disturbed an intruder hiding in the garden.

"You're welcome, but Daisy, don't try to track down the barmaid by yourself. We've got a team of professionals to do that. Anything you find out, you bring to me. I don't want you putting yourself in harm's way."

"I won't." She fiddled in her purse for her house keys. The snow was beginning to settle on the ground and her breath came out in a fine mist.

"I'm serious, Daisy," McGuinness called through the open car door. "She could be the murderer."

"So could Hannah or Clive," she retaliated. "Or both of them."

"Yes, and we will continue to investigate until we get to the bottom of it."

"Are you going to re-search Holly Lodge?" She paused before closing the door. Snowflakes were sticking to her hair and coat.

"Yes, I think we must. Just in case there's another body buried there. I'll get the K-9 unit in tomorrow. If there's someone there, the dogs will find them."

Daisy shivered as a wet snowflake slipped down the back of her collar. The weather was deteriorating fast and McGuinness still had to drive back to Guildford. "Drive safely, Paul."

"I will. Take care, Daisy. See you soon."

He waited until she was safely inside before he drove away.

Chapter 7

"Of course I knew Thomas Pierce," spluttered Liz Roberts the following day. She'd popped into the salon under the pretense of making an appointment to have her nails done, but Daisy suspected she just wanted to catch up on the latest developments in the case. "Don't tell me it was his body you found at Holly Lodge?"

"I'm afraid it was," Daisy replied. The next of kin had been notified, so she assumed it was safe to tell people about it, although most of the community knew already. That was the problem with small towns: Nothing stayed secret for long. "How did you know him?"

"He was a big donor for a charity in Esher. Rising Star, I think it was called. They help talented kids from disadvantaged backgrounds. It's a very worthy cause. We'd met a couple of times at various local events." Liz and her husband, Roy, were involved with several high-profile charities. She shook her head and a scattering of snowflakes fell from her faux fur headband onto the floor. "We all thought he'd run off with the barmaid from the Coach and Horses."

Daisy stared at her. "You knew about his affair?"

"Oh, yes. Everybody did, except his poor wife, of course. The spouse is always the last to know." Her mouth thinned into a hard line. Liz had found herself in that same boat earlier in the year, but she'd since reconciled with her husband. For someone of Liz's standing in the community, divorce was not an option. Her words.

"Did you know her? The barmaid, I mean?" Daisy's pulse kicked up a notch.

"Gosh, no." Liz pulled a face like she'd eaten something rancid. "I don't frequent the Coach and Horses, although Roy has been a few times with his golfing buddies. I could ask him if he remembers her."

"That would be useful," Daisy said. "I know the police are trying to trace her, so any information you can give would be appreciated."

"I doubt Roy knows her whereabouts, but I'll see what I can find out." She gave Daisy a conspiratorial wink. "Anything to help your handsome detective."

"Oh, he's not my—"

Krish came bounding over. "Dais, I need your help with Yvette's color. Penny's double-booked and Ruth from the doctor's office is here for her hair straightening. I've already applied the tint and she's been under the dryer for ten minutes. Can you take over?"

"Sure." Daisy turned to Liz. "I'm sorry, Liz. I have to go, but do let me know if you find out anything."

Liz patted her arm. "You know I will, dear." And she swanned out into the unyielding snow.

"What was that about?" asked Yvette, the owner of the chic French boutique next door to the salon as Daisy led her from the dryer to a chair in front of a gilded mirror. Her skin was pink from the heat and her hair was wrapped in foils.

"Oh, Liz recalled meeting the man who was found dead at Holly Lodge. Apparently, he was involved with a charity in Esher. Rising Star, I think she said. Have you heard of it?"

"Terrible business, that," murmured Yvette with a little shake of her head. As usual, she was immaculately attired in a seasonal red knitted dress with a navy-blue belt around her slender waist, and a matching handbag, stashed under the chair at her feet. "I can't say that I have."

Daisy pushed on. "The whole town thought he'd run off with a barmaid from the Coach and Horses, a woman called Lilly Rosewood." Daisy usually soaked up gossip, not spread it, but she was desperate to find out if any of her customers knew where Lilly was. She wasn't actively looking for her, she was merely inquiring.

Yvette glanced up. "Lilly Rosewood?"

"Yes, did you know her?" Daisy's heart skipped a beat.

"Actually, I think I did. Was she a petite brunette, always smiling?"

"I didn't know her," admitted Daisy. She hadn't even seen a photograph of Thomas Pierce's mistress.

"If it is the same woman I'm thinking of, she used to buy her scarves at my boutique. I sold her several over the years."

"You wouldn't happen to have an address for her, would you?" It was a long shot, but Yvette might just have something on file.

"I can look," she offered. "But most of my customers pay by card so I don't take their address down."

"Even her card details would help," said Daisy hopefully, although McGuinness could probably get those himself.

"Okay, I'll see what I can find."

Daisy checked Yvette's color and dispensed her to the basin so that Bianca could rinse out the tint. That gave her five minutes in which to ring McGuinness. Outside, a thick layer of powder had encrusted the pavement, so she went into the kitchenette to make the call instead.

"Rising Star, you say?" McGuinness's coarse voice filtered down the line.

"Yes, it's a charity in Esher."

"Daisy, I thought I told you not to get involved." He sounded weary. She wondered if he'd gone back to the station last night after dropping her off.

"You told me not to look for Lilly Rosewood," she clarified. "And I haven't. Although Yvette from the boutique next door said Lilly used to be a customer of hers. She's going to go through her records to see if she can locate an address. It might be a good place to start."

"I'm working on that," he said tightly.

"I know, but it can't hurt, right?"

He sighed. "Just be careful and let me know the minute you find anything—before you get it into your head to track her down."

"I will. Are you going to pay Rising Star a visit?" she asked hopefully.

"I will once I've looked into them." His tone lightened. "Since it's your lead, would you like to come with me? In an official capacity, of course."

She grinned. "I thought you'd never ask. What time?"

"How does three o'clock sound?"

Daisy rearranged the booking schedule in her head. If she could get Penny to cover her three o'clock appointment, she could take her six o'clock and let the senior stylist go early.

"Perfect. See you then!"

The Rising Star charity was located in a double-story Victorian terrace house off the bustling High Street in Esher. The name of the organization was written in gold lettering on a sign above the glossy black front door, along with a logo of a shooting star. It was simple, but effective.

They were let in by a smiling receptionist, who told them to please take a seat and Mr. Lightman would be with them shortly. Daisy was impressed by the office's classy interior decor. The downstairs living room had been converted into a waiting room with dark wooden floorboards polished to a high shine, a modern, swirling light fixture with a chrome finish attached to a suitably high ceiling, and a mahogany desk to one side where the receptionist sat, partially obscured by an enormous vase of pink and white roses interspersed with baby's breath. After a quick telephone call, a suave, handsome man in his late forties appeared out of an attached office.

"Hello, Bas Lightman." He held out a hand. They both stood up and shook it, McGuinness first, then Daisy. Lightman's gaze lingered on Daisy for a fraction longer than what was appropriate. "What can I do for you, detectives?"

"Oh, no. I'm not—" Daisy began.

McGuinness cut in. "I'm DCI McGuinness and this is Daisy Thorne, a consultant for Guildford CID."

Daisy was getting used to being called a consultant. It had a good ring to it. She looked at Lightman. "We want to speak to you in connection with Thomas Pierce. I believe you knew him?"

His eyes grew wide and his eyebrows shot up. "Thomas Pierce. Heavens, it's been years since I've heard that name."

"I believe he was a donor?"

"Yes, yes he was." He gestured to his office. "Please come in and we'll talk."

They followed him into the adjourning office with the same high ceilings, but in place of the bright, modern light fixture, he'd opted for subdued spot lighting. A lamp on a dark wooden sideboard sent a rosy glow over the room while an angular desk lamp shone a brighter, white light onto a pile of paperwork he was going through. A gold pen lay on top of the pile.

He gestured to two leather-backed chairs opposite his desk. "Please, take a seat. Can I get you anything? Coffee, tea? Rachel makes a great espresso." He grinned, showing an array of startlingly white teeth.

McGuinness and Daisy sat down. "No, we're good, thanks," McGuinness replied. Personally, Daisy would have loved an espresso, but she kept her mouth shut. They had more important things to focus on.

Lightman took his time getting comfortable, all the while keeping the suave smile in place. He reminded

Daisy of a smooth-talking, well-groomed salesman, but she had to admit, he was charming.

"Now, what is it you want to know?"

"When last did you see Thomas Pierce?" McGuinness got straight to the point. He wasn't one for small talk.

"Hmm . . . let's see. It's been a while." He tilted his head back. "Maybe two years ago, when he disappeared with that bar girl and left his wife and daughter behind. Not very sporting of him, if you get my drift." He shook his head disapprovingly. Daisy glanced around the room and saw several framed photographs of Lightman with celebrities and politicians. He had his arm around the prettier ones.

"You mean Lilly Rosewood?" McGuinness inquired.

He shrugged. "I didn't know her name. I just heard via the rumor mill, you know. Although, it was quite strange."

"What was?" Daisy asked.

"The way he left. It was very sudden, you see. He'd volunteered to be Father Christmas at our annual Christmas charity event—it's one of our biggest fundraisers of the year. Except he didn't turn up. The children were bitterly disappointed. I must say, he let us down very badly." He shook his head somberly. "I had to get one of the elves to hand out the presents instead, but it wasn't the same. Thomas had this larger-than-life quality about him that the children loved."

"I'm afraid I have some bad news," McGuinness said.

Lightman glanced up. "What's that?"

"Thomas Pierce didn't run away, he was murdered. We found his body in an empty property near Cobham two days ago."

Lightman stared at them. Daisy swore the color drained

from his face. "Murdered?" he repeated. There was no ar-
rogance in his tone now.

McGuinness's eyes never left his face. "Yes. He died
from a blow to the head."

"Well, I'll be . . ." He leaned back in his chair, a
shocked expression on his face. "All this time I thought
he'd done a runner. I have to admit, it was odd the way he
let us down like that. Not really in his character. He was
very dedicated to the charity."

"In what way?" asked Daisy.

"What?" Lightman still seemed miles away.

"In what way was he dedicated? Was he involved in
other events as well as the Christmas fundraiser?"

"Oh, yes." Lightman shook his head as if to clear it.
"He gave generously, but at the same time he really cared
about the kids. He was on our organizational team as a
volunteer and was involved with the grassroots football
team. We were sad to see him go."

"How big were his donations?" McGuinness asked.

Lightman shifted in his chair. "They were fairly siz-
able. He was one of our more prolific donors."

McGuinness leaned forward. "Would you mind if we
took a look at your donor records?"

Lightman shifted uncomfortably in his chair. "I'm not
sure about that. Many of our donors are wealthy individuals who wouldn't want their details to be given out. I
have a responsibility to maintain their privacy."

"We can get a warrant and come back," McGuinness
said. "But then we'll be taking all your laptops and other
documentation with us. It would save time and considerable inconvenience if you complied with us now."

The suave demeanor changed to one of annoyance, but

he stood his ground. "I'm sorry, Detective, you will need to get a warrant if you want to see my records. I owe my donors that much."

Or yourself, Daisy thought, watching him squirm. What was it that he didn't want them to see?

McGuinness wasn't fazed. "If that's the way you want to play it, Mr. Lightman, that's fine by me. We'll be back when we have a warrant. Thank you for your time."

Daisy, however, was less patient. "He's hiding something," she said as soon as they got outside.

"If he is, we'll find out what it is when we get access to his accounts."

"What if he destroys his records? A warrant will take time and we've given him ample warning that we're coming back."

"He can't hide his bank transactions," McGuinness replied. "If they don't match up to his ledgers, we'll know he's fudged the books and we'll get him for fraud on top of anything else he might be guilty of."

Daisy grimaced. "I hope you're right."

Chapter 8

Esher High Street was teeming with festive shoppers. The Christmas lights in the shape of Santa on his sleigh twinkled merrily and everywhere people carried colorful bags and packages. Once again, the traffic was going at a snail's pace, but this time it was because of the number of people, rather than the snow, which was still falling in light, fluffy flurries.

As they passed a coffee shop, Daisy said, "Do you mind if we pull over here? I'd love to get a treat for the crew at Ooh La La. They've been working so hard lately, especially covering for me."

"Good idea." McGuinness pulled over into a loading zone and turned off the engine. "I could use some sustenance myself. I skipped lunch." Parking at random was another perk of being a detective.

They went inside, where the aroma of coffee beans and gingerbread assailed them. "Aah," breathed Daisy. "It smells just like Christmas."

McGuinness seemed startled. "I almost forgot. I've been so busy working."

"Never be too busy to smell the coffee beans," she joked, joining the queue. "Actually, I haven't even got a tree yet. I keep meaning to get one, but then something always comes up, and now with all this snow . . ." She glanced out of the window at the snow-covered pavement. "I don't know when I'll get a chance to take the car out."

"I'm guilty of that too," he admitted with a small shrug. "The whole festive season seems to have passed me by this year."

"It's a shame," replied Daisy. "Christmas is my favorite time of year."

They got to the front and ordered their coffees. While they were waiting, McGuinness said, "I did some digging into Thomas Pierce and I couldn't find any records on him that go back further than three years ago."

"Three years? That would have been a year before he and Clive opened the real estate agency together."

"Exactly. He opened a bank account in Edgemead that same year and applied for a driver's license, but before that, nothing. It's like he didn't exist. I couldn't find any records on him at all, not even a social media profile."

Daisy frowned. "Do you think he changed his name?"

"That's the most likely scenario. I'm going to have to do some more digging. It's not illegal to change your name, but he seems to have created an entirely new life for himself."

"That does sound suspicious," Daisy agreed. They got

their coffees and went back to the car. McGuinness held the door open for her as she got in, careful not to topple the four cups in the cardboard holder. "What about his wife, Hannah?" she asked. "Did she also only materialize three years ago?"

McGuinness pulled out into the crawling traffic. "She checks out fine. Before she moved to Esher with Thomas Pierce, she lived in Glasgow. I can trace her right back to primary school. No problems there." Daisy remembered her saying as much when they'd spoken to her before.

"Maybe she can shed some light on her late husband's makeover?" Daisy suggested.

McGuinness turned to face her. "How about paying her a little visit, since we're in the neighborhood?"

"Now?" She glanced at the hot coffees on her lap.

He nodded. She was torn. "I'd love to," she said honestly. "But I've got to get back to the salon. I promised Penny I'd do her six o'clock shift and lock up."

He didn't react. "No worries. I'll drive you back."

The traffic was beginning to back up on the road to Edgemead and the continuously falling snow didn't help. Motorists were extra-cautious, which made the traffic crawl along at a glacial pace. It would take him a good half an hour to get her back to the salon and then he'd just have to turn around and come straight back again.

"Why don't you drop me here?" she said suddenly. "I'll take an Uber back."

He glanced across at her. She could see he wanted to do the chivalrous thing and drop her off at the salon, but the thought of the long drive there and back was making him hesitate. "Are you sure?"

"Of course." She glanced at the coffees. "I've got a gingerbread latte to keep me company and there should be an Uber around, or if not, I'll grab a taxi. There's a rank by the station a little further down."

"I'll drop you at the station, then. Thanks, Daisy."

"No problem. You don't want to have to come all the way back in this weather. It doesn't look like it's going to let up anytime soon." When she'd woken up this morning, the town had been covered in a thick blanket of snow. The main roads had since been cleared, but everything else looked like something out of a fairy tale.

He pulled over opposite Esher railway station and she made to get out of the car when she felt his hand on her arm. "Daisy, let me make it up to you. Are you free for dinner tonight?" Something in his voice made her turn to face him. His eyes held hers and she felt her pulse quicken. A cozy supper with Paul would be amazing. They hadn't gone out on a date for a long time, not since before she'd been arrested. She was beginning to wonder if theirs was just a platonic relationship and she'd imagined all the heated glances and awkward silences.

Then, her heart sank as she remembered a prior engagement. "I'm sorry, Paul. I can't do tonight. Floria's invited me to Brompton Court for supper. Can we take a rain check?"

He dropped his gaze. "Sure, no problem. We'll touch base tomorrow."

"Okay, good."

She watched his car drive off, his wide shoulders silhouetted against the windshield. There would be other opportunities to go out with Paul. Hopefully. Maybe. Her stomach fluttered at the thought.

* * *

"You are a saint!" Krish fell on the gingerbread latte in ecstasy.

"I needed this," said Penny with a grin. "It's been full-on since you left."

"Thanks, Daisy," called Asa from the nail bar. She had one lady with her fuchsia talons under a mini-dryer, another sitting in front of her with her fingers soaking in a bowl of warm water, and one more picking out a color from the array of varnish pots displayed on tiny shelves along the wall.

"Poor Asa hasn't even had time to go to the bathroom," whispered Krish. "Everybody waited until this week to have their nails done so they wouldn't chip before Christmas."

"We might have to think about getting her an assistant, if this carries on," mused Daisy as she checked the appointment book. She'd ended up catching the train back to Edgemead rather than taking a taxi. It was quicker at this time of the day. With the relentless snow and all the Christmas shoppers, the traffic was dire and Edgemead was only one stop away by rail. Besides, she'd enjoyed admiring the snowy scenery out of the windows.

"Yes, please," replied Asa, who had supersonic hearing.

Daisy had two more appointments and then with Krish's help, tidied the salon and readied it for the following day. While they were working, he demanded to know everything that had happened in the investigation so far. Daisy gave him a watered-down version, knowing that anything she said would be all over the village by nightfall. Krish's insatiable need to gossip had got him into trouble before, but it appeared there was no changing him.

"Thomas Pierce must have done something really bad if he changed his name." Krish swept up the hair on the floor. "I mean, why else would you move counties and assume a new identity?"

He had a point. Daisy stopped cleaning the mirrors and turned to him. "Or he had some unsavory people after him and he wanted to get away from them."

Krish gasped. "Maybe he was a gambler and owed people money, or perhaps he was part of an organized crime group."

"Anything's possible," Daisy acknowledged. "We won't know until DCI McGuinness speaks to his ex-wife. Hopefully she can shed some light."

"She must know what her husband was into," said Krish, eyes bright with excitement. "If she says she doesn't, she's lying."

"If anyone can find out the truth, it's DCI McGuinness," Daisy mused.

Krish chuckled. "I have to agree with you there. As dishy as he is, I've never felt so uncomfortable in my life as when he interrogated me earlier this year. He certainly has that intimidating glare down, doesn't he?"

Daisy smirked. "That he does."

"In fact, you're the only one who can stand up to him, Dais." He winked at her. "Or the only one he'd let stand up to him."

"Don't be silly," Daisy chastised. "He's like that with everyone."

"Uh-uh." He shook his head. "He allows you a lot of leeway. It's obvious he likes you, Dais. I wish you guys would get it together already."

"Stop it, Krish." Daisy shot him a stern look, but he

only threw back his head and laughed. "You don't fool me, Daisy Thorne."

When the workstations were clean and the floor swept, Daisy took off and left Krish to lock up. She was due at Brompton Court at seven, and she wanted to go home and change.

Brompton Court, an elegant country mansion and a classic example of eighteenth-century Palladian architecture, shimmered under a blanket of snow. The windows burned with a warm, yellow glow, while the outdoor lamps beneath the portico gave the four pillars a rather majestic appearance. Daisy walked up the stairs feeling like a minor royal, a sensation she always got when entering the grand mansion. Unfortunately, it no longer exuded the lush opulence of its past, and had instead become slightly shabby, but it was still awe-inspiring.

Violeta, the housekeeper, answered the door. "Daisy, dear, it's so nice to see you. Come in, the others are in the drawing room."

She made her way through the spacious hallway, her heels clicking on the Italian marble flooring, which although stylish, had lost its sheen and was chipped in places. She gazed up at the dusty chandelier, and then the life-size painting of Serena, Floria's mother, which hung above the grand staircase, her eyes watching you wherever you went.

Laughter emanated from the drawing room. Daisy pushed open the door and found Floria and her two half-sisters, Mimi and Donna standing together by the window. Floria's husband, Josh, was also there, playing snooker with Greg, Donna's husband, the family attorney.

The balls clashed and Josh yelled, "Gotcha!"

Greg put down his cue in defeat. "Lucky shot."

"No way! That was pure skill."

Greg laughed and put his hands up. "I'll get you on the rematch."

"Sorry I'm late." Daisy held up the bottle of prosecco she'd brought with her. She'd rushed home to shower and change, but then spent a frustrating few minutes deicing her car, and then driving here through the thickening snow, taking extra care not to skid on the icy roads.

"Don't worry about it." Floria embraced her. "Anne-Marie and her husband aren't here yet, either. They've been delayed due to the weather."

"Oh, the Natural Trust lady?" She remembered her from the salon. She kissed Mimi and Donna hello, both of whom looked stunning in floor-length evening gowns, their hair styled in glamorous updos. Donna's dress was a classic 1930s-style gown, while Mimi's was svelte and clinging, with a slit up one side almost to her thigh. Floria looked incredible too, in a burgundy off-the-shoulder gown that emphasized her curves. Daisy, who'd been quite happy with her appearance when she'd left the house, suddenly felt very dowdy. It was easy to see Mimi and Donna were related: Both had witchy-green eyes and dark hair that they'd inherited from Serena, along with their musical talent. Floria was the odd one out with pale blond curls and big, blue eyes. In fact, Floria and Daisy looked more alike than Floria and her half-sisters.

"Yes, I thought I'd invite her and her husband over so they can get a better look at the place."

"I can't believe you never told me you were thinking about selling Brompton Court."

"Oh, didn't I? Sorry, Dais, I thought I had." Floria shook her head. "I've been so busy lately, it must have skipped my mind."

"That's my fault," said Mimi. "I've been occupying all of her time. I must say, Daisy, it's lovely to see you again, particularly without the dead body in the room."

Daisy laughed. "I hope you weren't too traumatized by the experience."

Mimi shook her head. "Nothing a hot bath and a rest couldn't cure."

"I heard about what happened," Donna said. "How awful."

Daisy hugged her. Out of all three of Floria's half-sisters, Donna was the only one who lived in England. Mimi would be flying back to Australia with her husband once her UK tour was over, and Carmen, who Daisy had only met once several years ago at Serena's funeral, lived in Barcelona, where she was an up-and-coming opera singer like her late mother.

"It was a bit of a shock," Daisy said, "But the police are investigating now. They've managed to identify the victim. His name was Thomas Pierce from Esher."

"Thomas Pierce." Floria crinkled up her forehead. "I don't think I knew him."

"No, me neither," Daisy confessed. "It seems not many people did." She didn't mention his name change or lack of personal history.

"Let me take that." Josh took the bottle out of her hand. "Can I pour you a glass?"

"Yes, please, Josh."

Donna's husband, Greg, sidled up and put an arm around his wife's waist. "Hello, Daisy. It's good to see you again. Been staying out of trouble?"

Floria chuckled. "That'll be the day! She's in it up to her neck with this murder at Holly Lodge."

Greg shook his head. "Curiosity killed the cat, you know, Daisy."

"It was also the driving force behind innovation," she replied lightly. "Anyway, don't worry, I'm not involved. I just helped DCI McGuinness with some profiling."

"Is that what they're calling it nowadays?" teased Josh with a lopsided grin. He handed her a glass of bubbles.

Daisy shot him a look as she accepted the glass. She didn't mind their teasing, although her more off-again than on-again relationship with McGuinness was not something she was ready to dissect. "Enough about me. Floria, what made you decide to sell Brompton Court?"

Her best friend sighed. "I don't know, Dais. I haven't made up my mind yet. I'm waiting for Anne-Marie to give me a good sales pitch, and then I'll see. On the one hand, I'd love to keep it in the family, but on the other, it's so expensive to run and nobody's ever here. Josh and I are in London most of the time and we don't come here as much as we used to, and Violeta wants to retire. It seems like the right time to pass it on to someone who will take care of it."

"At least the National Trust will restore it to its former glory," said Josh.

"It is a pity to see it going to ruin," added Greg, who as Dame Serena's attorney, had seen Brompton Court in its heyday. Daisy could see Floria was torn.

The doorbell rang and her hostess said, "That will be them now."

A short time later, Anne-Marie, resplendent in an emerald-green caftan, and her husband, a stocky man with a hard, but not unattractive face, were shown into the drawing room. Floria made the introductions and the men drew Andrew into conversation.

"Oh, Daisy, I didn't know you were a friend of Floria's," Anne-Marie said.

"Yes, we've known each other for years," Daisy admitted.

"You must have known the great Dame Serena Levanté, then." Anne-Marie gushed. "I am such a fan. I was telling Floria that I listen to her *Best of* album at least once a week."

"She was very talented," agreed Daisy, glancing at Floria, who very subtly rolled her eyes behind her guest's back. It was a well-known fact among Floria's friends that she and her mother had not got on.

"I would have loved to have seen Brompton Court when she was here," Anne-Marie went on. "I've heard stories about the lavish parties and glamorous guests."

"They're all true," confirmed Daisy with an enigmatic smile. She'd been to several of them herself and seen the guests in ball gowns swirling around the grand hall while Serena sang like a nightingale from her perch at the top of the staircase. Flanked by a world-class orchestra, her sublime voice had resonated around the vast room, giving everybody chills. No matter what people said about Serena, her talent had been undisputable. "It was quite a spectacle."

"Aah," sighed Anne-Marie. "Wouldn't it be nice to see it like that again? Often our National Trust properties are hired by wealthy individuals and companies for private and corporate events. It adds to our revenue," she confided to Floria, who looked shocked at the thought. "This would make a stunning wedding venue. Can you imagine getting married underneath a gazebo by the duck pond, with the reception in the grand hall? How romantic."

Floria glanced at Daisy in alarm. It was clear she needed a lot more convincing before she was going to hand over the keys to her family property.

"Supper's ready," announced Violeta, poking her head into the drawing room. "Please come through."

Floria had hired a caterer friend to do the cooking and the rich aroma of roasted lamb and mint jelly emanated from the dining room. They filed in and gathered around the enormous table. There was no formal seating arrangement.

"Just plonk yourselves anywhere." Floria waved her hands around. She wasn't one for traditions, preferring a carefree, easy approach to her own dinner parties. For her clients, however, she often organized glittering black-tie events where everything was planned down to the last detail.

"Oh, how wonderful," breathed Anne-Marie, taking it all in. Floria, true to form, had created a Christmas setting worthy of a magazine shoot. The red-and-green plaid tablecloth gave the room a festive feel, and the centerpiece was layered with branches of cypress, sprigs of boxwood, pinecones, and other natural elements. The ruby-red crystal wineglasses and red napkins contrasted vividly against the white dinner service. A pine wreath in the center housed a thick candle that flickered invitingly.

Daisy found herself opposite Anne-Marie, with Floria between them at the head of the table. Donna sat on her other side.

"You should have brought Paul," Floria whispered to her once they'd sat down.

Daisy blushed. "Oh, he's so busy with this case, he wouldn't have had time."

"Maybe next time, then," said Floria, with a wink.

Josh poured them all a glass of Cabernet Sauvignon, selected specifically to go with the slow-braised beef, and they dug in. The food was delicious. Floria's friend had really outdone herself, but then Floria knew how to cater a party. That was her business, after all.

"How is Prima Donna Productions doing?" Donna asked. Floria's business was organizing parties for the rich and famous, mostly musicians, thanks to her late mother's extensive network and Floria's own contacts from her previous job in PR.

"We've been very busy leading up to Christmas," she confessed. "But it's quieted down a bit now. I've got an important event on Boxing Day, but I'm free until then."

"She deserves a break." Josh smiled at his wife. "And it's nice to see something of her."

"Hear! Hear!" sang Mimi. "I'm so grateful you could spend some time with me, Flo. I really appreciate it."

"You know you're always welcome," replied Floria. "And soon Holly Lodge will be ready for you and Rob to move into."

"I can't wait," said Mimi. "Not that we don't appreciate your hospitality, but it's so nice having one's own things around."

"As soon as you're settled, your tour kicks off," Daisy added. "You must be so excited."

"Excited and nervous." She grimaced. "I suffer badly with nerves. I always have done."

"So do I," said Donna, who was an accomplished violinist. "But the more nervous I am, the better I play."

"Let's toast to Mimi's sold-out UK tour." Josh raised his glass.

"To Mimi's tour," they all said simultaneously and clinked glass.

"I've got tickets to the show in January," whispered Anne-Marie to Daisy. "I can't wait."

"We're all going," Daisy said. "It should be great fun."

Once again, Anne-Marie was adorned in costume jewelry. She had a long strand of fake pearls doubled around her neck and a hulking great emerald on the middle finger of her right hand. Although over-the-top, they seemed to work with the flowing green caftan, which Daisy noticed was decorated with a faint oriental design. There was also blue paint under her fingernails and a white smudge on her lower arm.

"Are you an artist?" Daisy asked, catching Anne-Marie admiring a copy of a Raphael on the dining room wall—at least she thought it was a copy. You never quite knew with Floria's family.

"Yes, how did you know?"

"Just a guess." Daisy smiled.

"It's only a hobby," confided Anne-Marie, flushing, "but I do so enjoy it. Andrew says I should try to sell my paintings, but that's not why I paint. He doesn't understand."

"It's a lovely hobby to have. We all need something we're passionate about."

"Exactly." Anne-Marie beamed. "Do you have a hobby?"

Did she? Daisy wasn't sure sleuthing was classed as a hobby; neither was gossiping or plying innocent customers for information. "I play the piano," she said vaguely.

Anne-Marie beamed. "I'd love to be musical, but unfortunately I'm completely tone-deaf. Can't tell an A from a D. I do admire people who play instruments and sing, like Dame Serena, for example. What a magnificent voice! And it seems her daughter, Mimi, has inherited her vocal talents."

"Donna's also very accomplished," said Daisy. "She plays first violin in the London Philharmonic."

Anne-Marie sighed. "Such a gifted family. Serena must have been so proud of them."

Daisy didn't respond. Serena hadn't acknowledged the existence of her three illegitimate daughters until after she'd passed away. Only Floria had grown up with her, and that hadn't been easy. But it wasn't her place to say, so she kept quiet and listened while Anne-Marie waxed lyrical about Serena and a concert of hers she'd been to in the nineties.

She wondered what McGuinness was doing. Was he still at the office? Had he spoken to Hannah Collington again, and what had she said about her husband's name change?

Outside, it was still pelting down, so she couldn't nip out and call him for an update and when she finished dinner, it would be too late. There was nothing for it, she'd have to wait until morning. Curiosity was indeed killing her, but not in the way Greg had insinuated. Grinding her teeth, she went back to the conversation.

Chapter 9

Daisy woke up to a magical winter wonderland. The meadow across the road was completely covered by a blanket of snow, the trees glistened white in the morning sun—even the wooden turnstile looked like it belonged on a Christmas cake.

"Wow," she breathed, staring out of the bedroom window. Detective McGuinness should have taken that bet. It was looking very likely that they'd have a white Christmas.

She trudged down the lane to the High Street in her Wellington boots, carrying her smart court shoes, along with her purse, in a carrier bag slung over one shoulder. The snow made it hard to walk and she stumbled many times before she got there, but she didn't mind. It was so beautiful and her winter coat was warm and the woolen scarf she wore—a gift from Yvette for her last birthday—prevented the cold from stealing down her neck. As she walked, she breathed in the frigid air and felt her airways tingle.

"Isn't it stunning?" Penny met her outside Ooh La La. The senior stylist had come from the station and left a trail of Ugg boot prints along the pavement behind her. Her cheeks were flushed and clashed wonderfully with her red hair. "It's like the snow has covered all the ugliness and the world is pure again."

If only it was so, Daisy thought, unlocking the door to the salon. It was freezing inside but she soon got the central heating going, while Penny put on the kettle.

"I met Yvette for a drink yesterday," Penny called from the kitchenette. "She said to tell you she had an old credit card slip with Lilly Rosewood's details on it, but no address."

"Thanks," replied Daisy, joining her. "I'm sure DCI McGuinness will trace her via her bank records anyway. It was a long shot."

"If this Lilly woman didn't run away with your murder victim, then where do you think she is?" Penny set about making coffee.

"I honestly have no idea." Daisy gnawed on her lower lip. "She may be dead for all we know."

Penny glanced up in alarm. "Do you really think so?"

"It's possible. If she was with Thomas Pierce when he went missing, she might also have been killed. Why else would she disappear?"

"Yes," murmured Penny. "Even if she was having an affair with him, there would be no reason to disappear unless she was involved in his death."

"Which is why we need to find her." Daisy leaned

against the countertop. "If she didn't kill her lover, she might know what happened to him. Maybe she saw something and that's why she went into hiding."

"Heavens." Penny wrapped her hands around her mug. "Poor woman. Imagine being so scared you have to hide away for years. How awful."

"Well, if we—I mean, if DCI McGuinness catches whoever did this, Lilly will be free to live her life again."

"If she's not the killer," Penny added with a shiver.

"My shoes were not made for this weather," moaned Asa as she burst through the door accompanied by a flurry of snowflakes. "They're soaked." She squelched across the floor to the nail bar.

"Whoa!" Daisy ran out of the kitchenette. "Stay there and I'll bring you a cloth. Take your shoes off and leave them under the radiator to dry. We can't have you dripping all over the floor. It's hazardous for the customers."

Asa took off her shoes and padded over to the nearest radiator. She placed her shoes on the floor under it, then turned around so her legs were backed against it. "Aah." She closed her eyes in ecstasy. "That's better."

Daisy used the toweling cloth to wipe up the puddles left in Asa's wake and then tossed it to her. "Here, dry off and keep your feet on the towel so they don't freeze."

"Thanks, Daisy."

They all jumped as there was a loud crash against the glass frontage of the shop.

"Oh my goodness!" Daisy rushed toward the door as she realized what had happened. An old woman had slipped on the icy pavement and fallen against the window, her walking stick clattering against the glass. Luckily, Krish had been bounding up the road and was already helping her to her feet. She appeared a bit dazed, but otherwise uninjured.

"Are you okay?" Daisy rushed out to help. She took the woman's other arm. It felt frail beneath her own. "That was quite a fall."

The old woman took a moment to compose herself. "Yes, thank you, dear. How silly of me. It's this snow, you know. It's so easy to lose one's footing."

"It is," said Daisy worriedly. "Are you sure you're okay?" The woman was quite fragile and she had taken a bad tumble. Perhaps they should check she hadn't broken anything.

"I think I'm okay, dear. If I could just sit down for a moment, I'll let you know."

"Of course." Daisy and Krish helped her into the hairdressing salon and eased her down onto the velvet sofa. "Where is my stick?" She glanced worriedly toward the door.

"I've got it," Penny said, holding it up. The floor was soaked again as the clumps of snow they'd trailed in melted in the warmth. She passed the walking stick to the old lady, whose hands were shaking. The poor woman had got more of a fright than she was letting on.

"Penny, won't you make this lady some sweet tea?" Penny, who'd also noticed the trembling, disappeared to the kitchenette.

"Thank you, dear," she muttered. "A cup of tea would be lovely. Just what the doctor ordered."

"I'm Daisy." Daisy sat down beside her. "This is my salon."

"My name is Barbara, but you can call me Babs."

"Well, I'm glad you're all right, Babs," Daisy said with a smile. "You had a nasty fall."

"The snow cushioned me," she said. "Otherwise, I might have really hurt myself."

"Are you alone?" Daisy asked. "Is there anyone I can call to come and pick you up?"

"Oh, I'm with my daughter, Philippa. She's in the pharmacy across the road picking up my prescription. She'll be along in a minute."

"Okay, that's good. When you see her, let me know and I'll pop out to call her. I don't think you should be walking by yourself in this weather. It's very dangerous and you're still a bit shaken up."

Babs responded by patting her on the hand. Daisy admired her spirit.

Customers started to arrive and before long, Daisy, Penny, and Krish were attending to cuts, highlights, and blow-dries, while Asa painted a young woman's nails fire-engine red.

"That's my daughter," Babs called out, causing Daisy to put down her scissors and turn around. A slender woman with wispy blond hair was crossing the road, a package under one arm and an oversized handbag over the other. She was looking around, like she'd lost something.

Daisy poked her head out the door. "Excuse me, your mother's in here. She had a fall."

"Oh, no!" The woman darted across the road, narrowly avoiding a bus. "Is she all right?"

"She's fine, just a little shaken up." Daisy stood back to let her enter the salon. She really must get a doormat for inside the entrance.

"Oh, Mum. Are you okay?" Her daughter sat down beside her. "I told you to wait for me."

"I know, dear. Don't fret. I'm fine."

"He left behind a wife and a young daughter." Krish's voice rang out over the hair dryer. "The wife's name is Hannah Collington."

Daisy had told her team it was okay to chat about the murder in case anyone knew the victim, or even better, his lover, Lilly Rosewood, although Krish didn't need any encouragement. So far, they'd had no luck. It seemed Thomas Pierce hadn't been in the area long before he'd been killed and consequently none of the locals knew him.

"Did he say Hannah Collington?" Philippa asked, glancing at Daisy.

"Yes, he did. Do you know her?"

"I used to," Philippa said with a small smile. "Our daughters went to the same nursery school. She was Hannah Pierce back then, but I remember her well. Her daughter Elly was friendly with my daughter, Zoe."

Daisy caught her breath. She sat down on the footstool opposite Philippa. Who said gossiping didn't pay off? "Did you know her around the time her husband disappeared?"

"Why, yes, I did. What an awful business that was. I felt so sorry for her. I think everyone did. There were rumors that he'd run off with someone else."

"Except he didn't." Daisy leaned forward. "He was found murdered at Holly Lodge a few days ago. His body had been there for nearly two years."

Philippa grimaced. "I had heard, yes. It's terrible to think he's been dead all this time. Luckily, Hannah had Clive. He was marvelous with Elly. He used to come to the school to collect her after Tom disappeared. I think Hannah was too embarrassed to face anyone, not that I blame her."

Daisy nodded in agreement. It was hard enough telling her friends that Tim had left, and they hadn't been married, nor did they have any kids together.

"She married Clive soon afterward, didn't she?"

"Yes. Clive was always sweet on her, even before Tom disappeared."

Daisy's breath caught in her throat. "Really? Did you know Clive well?"

Philippa raised her eyebrows. "Why yes, he sold us our house in Esher. We've since moved to Edgemead, but back then we lived near to the village green. It was a lovely part of the county. I miss it." Close to where Hannah and Clive lived now.

"Were they seeing each other when Thomas was still around?" Daisy asked cautiously. She was pushing it, but if there was a chance that the two had been having an affair before her husband went missing, it would add to their motive.

"Oh, I wouldn't know," Philippa said quickly, but she wouldn't meet Daisy's eye. "I'm not one to gossip."

That was a pity, but Daisy sensed she wanted to talk. "No one would blame her if she was," she said quietly. "From what I've heard, her husband didn't treat her very well. Apparently, he had something of a roving eye."

"Yes, there was that." Philippa wavered. "I don't suppose it matters now that he's dead . . ." She dropped her voice conspiratorially. "You were right. Hannah and Clive were having an affair. I know because she asked me to cover for her once." Her eyes grew wide. "But you didn't hear it from me."

"Of course not," Daisy said quickly. Wow, so Hannah and Clive were having an affair! And it had started before Thomas disappeared.

She glanced across at her customer still waiting in front of the mirror. She had to get back to work. "Thanks for talking to me, Philippa. I hope your mother is okay. She may have a bit of a bruise where she fell."

"I'll keep an eye on her," Philippa said, and helped her mother off the sofa.

Daisy's mind went into overdrive. What she'd discovered opened up a whole host of possibilities. Were they in it together? Had Clive killed Thomas because he wanted Hannah for himself? Had Hannah killed her husband to get rid of him so she could marry Clive? Was there some sort of altercation over Hannah's affair and it had got out of hand? Daisy opened the door so Philippa and Babs could leave, the questions swirling around in her mind, much like the snow outside.

Chapter 10

As soon as she had a break, Daisy rang McGuinness, but his phone went straight to voice mail. She fired off a text saying she had some news for him, then got to work on her next customer. By closing time, she still hadn't heard back. He must be busy following up his own leads. She wondered if he'd found Lilly Rosewood yet.

It was dark when Daisy finally locked up and stepped out into the High Street. The Christmas lights strung across the road sparkled merrily and she could hear carols emanating from the church on the corner. She walked home, careful not to slide on the slippery ice, but for the most part, the snow hadn't melted and the lane leading to her cottage, as well as the meadow, were still pristine and undisturbed. It was bitterly cold, and the air had that snowy tang that usually meant more was on the way.

"Hello, Frank," she called as she passed the village florist heading the other way. He was probably going up to the pub to meet his mates for a pint.

"Hello, Daisy. I haven't seen a tree in your front window this year."

She pulled a guilty face. "I know. We've been so busy at the salon, I haven't had a chance to get one and now it's probably too late." That and the murder had occupied all her time.

"That's a shame," he said and waved as he trudged on toward the Fox and Hound.

As she opened her garden gate, she heard a loud meow and saw her neighbor's cat, Mr. Tiddles, perched on the wall. His paws had left tiny cat prints in the snow.

"What are you doing outside?" Daisy murmured, as she walked past him toward her front door. Peering over the low wall into her neighbor's front yard, she noticed Moira's car was missing. He meowed again, then jumped down and squeezed past her into the house, his fur brushing softly against her legs.

She'd call Moira and let her know Mr. Tiddles was here. If she'd gone out yesterday, she may well be unable to get home because of the snow, and Mr. Tiddles didn't like being left alone. He was a social feline and probably the most popular tabby in the neighborhood. Moira was always updating her on his antics. She opened a can of tuna and turned it onto a side plate. Hopefully that would do, since she didn't have any cat food. There wasn't a meow of complaint from Mr. Tiddles. He fell on it with a swish of his tail and began eating it up.

"You must be hungry," Daisy observed fondly.

While the tabby ate, she stuck a frozen pizza in the oven, poured herself a glass of wine, then sunk down on the sofa to watch television. Channel Four were showing old reruns of her favorite detective drama, *Inspector Morse*. After a while, Mr. Tiddles came and curled up at her feet.

She was ten minutes into an episode, lost in the ancient Saxon architecture and Norman spires of Oxford, when her doorbell rang. "That'll be your mummy." She stroked the tabby's head, but when she opened the door, DCI McGuinness stood there, his broad frame obscuring the light from the overhead lamp.

"Paul, what are you doing here?"

"I got your message, so I thought I'd stop by. I hope I'm not intruding?" He glanced around as if expecting to find someone else in the house.

"Nope, it's just me. Oh, and Mr. Tiddles."

He frowned, then his gaze fell on the cat watching him warily from the foot of the couch. "The neighbor's?" he inquired. Daisy had mentioned Mr. Tiddles before.

"Yes, Moira isn't home. I've messaged her but she hasn't replied. She might be stuck somewhere on account of the weather."

"I know the feeling. I had to park in the High Street and walk here. Your lane is inaccessible. It's snowing again, by the way, so it's only going to get worse." McGuinness took off his coat, shook it out, and hung it on the hook beside the door. He handed her a carrier bag. "I bought muffins, freshly baked."

"Ooh, how nice!" Daisy put them on the kitchen counter. "From Paul's Bakery too. What a treat."

"They're from his last batch of the day."

He hovered halfway between the open-plan living room and the kitchen. Daisy gestured to the barstools beside the counter, which served as an eating area and separated the kitchen from the lounge. "Take a seat. I'm just about to have pizza if you want to join me? We can save the muffins for dessert."

He grinned. "Sounds good. I'm starving."

She poured him a glass of wine without asking, and he didn't refuse. His hair was messy and there were faint purple shadows under his eyes. He was working too hard as usual.

"I found out something today," she began.

He eased himself onto a barstool. "I'm all ears."

"It's an odd story, really," and she told McGuinness how Babs had fallen outside the shop and how her daughter, Philippa had come inside to fetch her.

"How is this relevant?" McGuinness asked.

"Well, it turns out that Philippa knew Hannah Collington back when she was still Hannah Pierce. Their children were at nursery school together. Anyway, she told me that Hannah and Clive were having an affair *while* she was still married to Thomas." She put her hands on her hips. "What do you make of that?"

"Well, well." McGuinness leaned back on his stool and studied her. "Is she sure? It's not just a rumor."

"She's sure. Hannah asked her to cover for her one night."

McGuinness tilted his head to the side. "That definitely gives them a motive, especially Hannah."

"I was thinking more along the lines of Clive," Daisy said. "Hannah is quite petite. I can't see her hauling her husband's body up the chimney, can you? Then she'd have to nail those boards in place. She doesn't fit the profile."

"Maybe she had help?" McGuinness suggested.

"Clive could have been her accomplice," Daisy argued.

McGuinness scratched his stubbly chin. "There's a problem with that theory. I sent Buckley up to Yorkshire to talk to Clive Collington's mother."

"She was in a home, wasn't she?" Clive had said he'd gone to his parents' for Christmas, but he could have been lying. With his father deceased and his mother incapacitated, it would be hard to prove.

"Yes, that's right. Well, it turns out her dementia is quite advanced. Buckley said she can't remember who visited her last week, let alone two years ago."

"Poor thing," mused Daisy. "That's so sad, but it does indicate that he could have been lying about being with them."

McGuinness watched as Daisy got the pizza out of the oven. "That smells good. I haven't eaten since breakfast."

"Doesn't the police station have a canteen?"

"Not one that I eat at." He pulled a face.

She laughed and placed it on a breadboard on the counter to cool, then she passed McGuinness the cutter. "Here, you do the honors, while I make us a salad."

He cut it into perfect triangles while she mixed lettuce, cucumber, tomato, and olives together in a bowl. Then she crumbled some feta cheese on top and stuck in two serving spoons.

"This is almost as good as Nonna Lina's," he said, referring to the Italian restaurant in Edgemead that Daisy liked to frequent.

"You'd never know it was store-bought," she said, grinning, drizzling some olive oil onto the salad. "Tuck in before it gets cold." He didn't need persuading and before long, the pizza and the salad were gone. McGuinness certainly had a healthy appetite.

"I'm sorry Buckley came back empty-handed." Daisy put the muffins on a plate. They were still warm and felt soft and bouncy beneath her fingertips.

"Actually, I was about to tell you—before you distracted me with food—that he spoke to the nurses at the care home and one of them remembered visiting Mr. and Mrs. Collington on Christmas Eve two years ago."

Daisy arched an eyebrow. "No way?"

"It's a small community. She worked for the National Health Service back then and since Mr. Collington was ill and Mrs. Collington was already becoming quite forgetful, their doctor had arranged for regular home checkups. She distinctly remembers Mr. Collington telling her that their son was coming to visit them on Christmas Day. The old guy was very excited about it."

Daisy paused, the muffin halfway to her lips. "Christmas Day? Didn't Clive say he drove up on Christmas Eve? If he didn't get there until Christmas Day, he has no alibi for the day of the murder."

McGuinness grinned. "Good memory. Yes, that's exactly what he said, so I had him brought in for questioning."

"You arrested him?" Daisy gasped.

"I questioned him under caution," McGuinness corrected, reaching for his wine.

"And?" Daisy stared at him, muffin forgotten. That's why he'd been out of touch all afternoon.

"Well, he had a perfectly logical explanation. He said he'd gone to a nearby village to look at a nursing home. He was thinking of moving his parents into one in the new year and was scouting the area. It was late, so he stayed overnight at a pub that rented out rooms, but he couldn't recall the name. The next morning, he went to his parents' house."

"Do you believe him?" Daisy resumed eating her muffin.

"I'm not sure, but since we don't have anything solid to hold him on, we had to release him while we verify his alibi. It would help if he could remember the name of the inn he stayed at." He rubbed his eyes.

"If he's telling the truth and he really is innocent, it's back to square one." Daisy collected the plates to put them in the dishwasher.

"Yep." He held her gaze. "But he could be making the whole thing up and he really left on Christmas morning to drive to his parents' place. That would have given him ample opportunity to lure Thomas Pierce to Holly Lodge in order to kill him."

Daisy shook her head. "If that's the case, I'm surprised Thomas fell for it. He knew Clive well; they were business partners. Surely he would have questioned meeting him at an abandoned property?"

"Clive could have arranged for him to meet a prospective buyer there," McGuinness pointed out. "Then when he arrived, it was Clive waiting for him."

"With a hammer," Daisy finished, cringing.

McGuinness frowned. "That's another thing. We don't have the murder weapon and we're not likely to ever find it, given the amount of time that's passed."

"Maybe you won't need it," Daisy said.

McGuinness shrugged. "We'll have to see what the team can find out. Otherwise, it's all just guesswork. The Crown prosecutor is never going to sanction an arrest based on what we have."

He was right. They needed concrete evidence before they could go for an arrest. "Have you managed to locate Lilly Rosewood yet?" Daisy asked, changing the topic. She brushed the remaining crumbs off the counter and into the bin.

"No, but we're working on it and we should have an address for her soon. No one can hide forever. There's always a trace."

"If she's still alive, you mean?" Daisy put in.

He leaned back and studied her. "We've got no reason to believe she's dead. The sniffer dogs went over Holly Lodge, including the grounds, and there's no trace of another body there."

"That's something, at least." The thought of two people being murdered at Mimi's new house was terrible and Daisy doubted the pop star would keep it, if that turned out to be the case. One dead body was bad enough.

"I've got an idea," Daisy said, once she'd finished clearing up. Mr. Tiddles was sound asleep on the sofa and outside, the snow was still falling.

"What?" He raised a suspicious eyebrow.

"It's nothing dangerous," she said, grinning. "Hang on, let me get my laptop."

She set it up on the counter and perched on the barstool next to him. "Now, where did you say Clive's parents lived?"

"Waverley, near Sheffield."

She pulled up Google Maps and searched for the Yorkshire town. "Let's have a look to see which villages are nearby."

"There are dozens," he pointed out. "This is what I've got my team working on. You don't need to do it, Daisy."

She ignored him. "How long did he say it took for him

to get from the inn to his parents' house the next morning?"

He blinked at her. "I didn't ask him that."

Daisy cocked her head to the side. "Perhaps you should."

McGuinness stared at her thoughtfully, then pulled out his mobile phone. Clive Collington took a while to answer and when he did, his voice was strained. McGuinness had put it on speaker so Daisy could listen in.

"Mr. Collington, it's DCI McGuinness here. I'm sorry for the late call. I'm trying to trace the pub you stayed at the night before Christmas two years ago. Could you give me an indication of how long the drive was to your parents' house the following day?"

There was a pause, then Clive said, "It wasn't long. Maybe twenty minutes."

"And you don't remember which direction you drove in?" McGuinness prompted.

"I was coming from the south," he replied. McGuinness studied the map. "Do any of these villages ring a bell? Troway? Birley Hay? Bramley? Stubley? Totley?"

"Totley sounds familiar," he interjected. "That could be it."

"You're sure?" asked McGuinness.

"Yes, yes. I think that was it. The care home I looked at was near Totley, I'm sure of it." The relief was evident in his voice. Daisy glanced at McGuinness. It seemed like Clive might have been telling the truth.

"Okay, thanks, Clive. We'll check it out and be in touch."

"Totley is a tiny village," Daisy pointed out, squinting at the map. "You have to zoom in just to see it." She enlarged the local area and added *pubs in Totley* to her

Google Map search. Little red teardrops popped up on the screen. "There are . . . eight pubs in the area."

"Only eight?" He gave a wry grin.

"It could be worse," she told him. "In some places there's a pub on every corner."

"True. Okay, you take those four and I'll take these four." He drew an imaginary horizontal line through the village.

Daisy picked up her phone off the counter and clicked on the first teardrop. The pub's details appeared in a panel on the left-hand side of the screen. She dialed the number, while McGuinness clicked on another teardrop and punched the number that came up into his phone. Given that it was late evening and prime pub-going hours, they should all be open.

Daisy waited while the phone rang. Whether anyone would hear the phone ringing, was a different matter. Eventually, a raspy female voice answered. Daisy inquired if they rented rooms above the pub and the woman said no.

"Did you ever have rooms above the pub?" she asked, thinking they may have discontinued them at some point in the last few years.

"No," the woman said, agitated. "We've never rented rooms above the pub. We're not that kind of establishment." And hung up.

McGuinness, who was still hanging on, raised an eyebrow. Daisy shook her head. "No luck."

She tried the next number. A male answered but it was so noisy in the background she could hardly hear him. She asked about rooms for rent and he too said they didn't do them and had never done.

With a sigh, she tried the third number. To her surprise,

a woman answered and there was no music, laughter, or noise in the background. Daisy explained what she was after and the woman said, yes, they did rent out rooms and when would she like to book?

"Oh, I'm not looking to reserve a room," Daisy explained. "I'm trying to find out whether a Mr. Clive Collington stayed there two years ago on Christmas Eve?"

There was a pause, and then the woman said, "I can't give you that information, I'm afraid. It's confidential."

"I'm working with the police," Daisy explained. "We're trying to verify an alibi. I can pass you over to the senior investigating officer if you'd prefer?"

A longer pause. Eventually, the woman said, "That's okay, hang on."

There was the sound of tapping on a computer. "Christmas Eve, you say? Two years ago?"

"That's right." Daisy held her breath.

"No, I'm sorry. We didn't have any visitors on December twenty-fourth two years ago. It's not a very popular night. Most people are at home with their families."

"You're sure?" Daisy asked.

"Yes, absolutely. There's nothing on the system."

"Okay, thank you," she said, disappointed.

McGuinness was shouting into the phone beside her. "Clive Collington! C-O-L-L-I-N-G-T-O-N." He rolled his eyes at her.

Daisy walked to the other side of the living room and tried the fourth number. It rang for ages, but eventually a man picked up. She repeated the question.

"Sorry, love," he said with a thick Yorkshire accent. "The inn isn't open over the festive season, just the pub.

No staff to manage it, you see. We close on the twentieth every year and don't open until the second January."

"Oh, I see. Thank you very much."

She hung up, feeling dejected. Maybe Clive had been lying and he hadn't stayed in Totley, or they'd got the town wrong. That was a possibility.

McGuinness was frowning. "You're sure?" he bellowed into the phone. Daisy perked up. Maybe he'd discovered something.

"Excellent, thank you." He hung up, a smug look on his face. "Bingo."

"You found it?"

"Yes. The inn is called the Cross Scythes. Collington was the only guest, which is why the landlady remembered him. He stayed one night and paid in cash."

Daisy pursed her lips. "It does sound plausible."

"He gave her his name so it's in the system. It's a good thing she logged the booking, otherwise there'd be no record of him having stayed there at all."

"Lucky for Clive," muttered Daisy. While she was glad they'd got a result, it did mean that Thomas's partner was off the hook.

"Well, that rules him out, then," said McGuinness. "I can tell my team to stop digging. It's one less thing for them to do."

He fired off a text message and then turned to Daisy. "Your idea paid off. Well done."

"I was only trying to help."

"Except now we're no closer to discovering who killed Thomas Pierce." He stifled a yawn. "I'd better get going, it's a long drive back to Guildford."

The detective lived half an hour's drive away in Surrey's largest town. This was where the Surrey police headquarters was situated, the center of crime-fighting in the county.

Daisy glanced at the time on the clock above the oven. It was half past nine. "Okay, but drive carefully, it's still coming down."

He peered through the window that looked across the road onto the meadow. Daisy hadn't drawn the blinds yet and the dark sky was hazy with diagonally driving snow. It wasn't far off from a blizzard. "It's got a lot heavier since I arrived."

"You're welcome to stay over," she offered, concerned. "The roads are going to be treacherous."

He hesitated.

"You can have the couch," she said quickly. "As long as you don't mind sharing with Mr. Tiddles, but don't worry, he is house-trained, despite his name."

He gazed at her. "I don't want to intrude."

"Oh, it's no bother, honestly. I'm going to head up to bed shortly anyway."

"What about your movie?" he asked, glancing to the television that was still on pause.

She waved a hand in the air. "Oh, don't worry about that. I wasn't going to finish watching it. Anyway, I'm exhausted." It wasn't a lie. She'd been working so hard, she couldn't wait to sink into her soft bed. If Paul hadn't come round, she'd probably have fallen asleep on the sofa already.

"In that case, Daisy, I might take you up on your offer. It's looking pretty dire out there."

She gave a nod, ignoring her racing pulse. "I'll just get you a pillow and some blankets."

"Thanks."

When she got back, he was sitting beside the big tabby, stroking his ears. The cat purred contentedly beside him. "It looks like you've made a friend," she commented, putting a pillow and a duvet on the free armchair.

"Are you sure you don't mind?" He glanced up.

"Of course not." Just then Daisy's phone beeped. "Oh, that's me."

She checked the screen. "It's Moira from next door. She's staying at her sister's in Notting Hill tonight and asked me to feed Mr. Tiddles."

"He's one step ahead of you," McGuinness remarked. He stood up to get the bedding and the cat jumped off and went to sleep on the vacant armchair.

"Okay, well, I'll leave you to it." Daisy hovered behind the couch, suddenly feeling awkward. Seeing Paul spread out on her sofa made her realize how much she'd missed having a man around. His presence was reassuring and even though she had no reason to feel afraid, she liked him being here.

"Good night, Daisy," he said, huskily.

"Good night, Paul." She darted up the stairs to bed.

Chapter 11

Daisy woke up to the sound of someone rummaging around downstairs. She sat up in bed, her heart thumping and looked around for the nearest weapon. There was someone in her house! Then she remembered Paul had stayed over last night and let out a slow, shaky breath.

She pulled on jeans and a sweater and made her way downstairs. To her surprise, the detective was folding up the duvet, wearing nothing but his trousers. She stared, torn between embarrassment that he was half-naked and mesmerized by his muscular torso and the fine smattering of hair that covered his chest. He glanced up and saw her.

"Good morning." He threw her a sheepish grin. "You caught me before I put my shirt on."

"Morning." Trying to act normally, she padded into

the kitchen and put on the kettle, but she kept her back to him so he wouldn't notice her hot cheeks. "Did you sleep well?"

"Better than I have in weeks," he admitted. "It's so quiet here."

"Yes, not many cars come down here, but then this is a very small lane and it doesn't really lead anywhere except to the river. Tea or coffee?" She refused to turn around until he had his shirt back on. Another glimpse of that manly chest and she might go weak at the knees.

"Coffee, thanks," he replied. She heard the sound of the blinds being drawn, followed by an expletive. "That's a lot of snow!"

She spun around. "Is it?" The meadow outside was completely covered. It was pristine and smooth like icing on a cake, with not a dent in it. "I hope you can get to your car?"

His eyes crinkled at the corners. "You don't have any skis, do you?"

At the look on her face, he chuckled. "Don't worry, I'll manage."

He joined her in the kitchen, which was hardly big enough for two people. Suddenly, she was very aware of his presence and it didn't help that every time she blinked, she saw an image of his naked torso.

"What can I do to help?"

"There's bread if you want some toast." She gestured to the bread bin on the counter.

"Sounds good." He got out two slices and dropped them into the toaster. Mr. Tiddles slunk between his legs, mewing. "Shall I let him out?" he asked, glancing down.

"Sure. He probably wants to go home, but he'll be

back when he's hungry. I'll get some cat food today in case Moira doesn't make it home tonight either. I can't see her driving back in this."

McGuinness opened the door and an icy gust blew in. The tabby dashed out, but feeling the snow underfoot, vaulted over the wall and into his own garden. McGuinness stepped outside and peered over. "He's gone in via the cat-flap."

As he closed the door, his phone rang. He pulled it out of his back pocket, shooting Daisy an apologetic glance. "DCI McGuinness."

Daisy noted how his tone changed from relaxed and casual to terse and professional, as if it was a suspect on the other end of the line.

"You have? Where?"

Daisy held her breath.

"Okay, text me the address. I'll get right over there."

"Did you find Lilly Rosewood?" she asked, as soon as he hung up.

"Yes, Buckley traced her credit card to an address in Borough, south London. Her surname has changed. It's Westerford now, so she may have got married."

"Makes sense," said Daisy. "That's why she was so hard to find."

"I'm going to head over there." He reached for his jacket, which was still hanging on the wall hook beside the front door and turned to face her. "Sorry to run out on you like this, but thanks for your hospitality. I appreciate it."

"Of course, it was a pleasure having you."

He met her gaze and there was a short pause. The toast popped up, making them jump.

"I'm surprised you haven't asked me if you can come along," he said, breaking the silence.

"That's because I can't." Daisy blew out her cheeks as she thought of the lost opportunity. "We're fully booked at the salon today. It's always crazy the week before Christmas, and we'll be flat-out like this until the twenty-third."

"You're closed on Christmas Eve?" he asked.

"Yes, by then we'll be worn out, and the team deserves some time off. It is Christmas, after all. We reopen on the twenty-seventh."

"I see."

"Do you have any plans over Christmas?" She kept her voice light.

"Not with this case still open and a killer out there," he replied.

"Well, I hope you'll be able to come to the Christmas market this Sunday?"

He hesitated, then said, "I'd like to, but it depends whether I can get away."

"You should try to come, it's great fun. There are stacks of stalls and a lovely, festive atmosphere."

"I'll try my best." He reached for the door.

"Hang on." She turned around and quickly buttered a slice of toast. "Here, take this with you. It'll be hard work trudging through the snow to your car. You'll need the sustenance."

"Thanks." He grimaced. "I hope I can find it under all this snow. If the roads are too bad, I'll take the train. It'll be easier."

"Okay, keep me posted."

His gaze lingered as he opened the door. "I will."

*   *   *

"He stayed over?" Krish exclaimed, a fraction too loudly. His ten o'clock appointment, an austere woman in a buttoned-up blouse, gave Daisy a sideways glance. It was the last Saturday before Christmas and they were chockablock the entire day.

"Not like that," she hissed. "He slept on the couch. We got snowed in."

"How convenient." Krish winked at her.

He really was incorrigible. "Anyway, they found Lilly Rosewood in south London, so he's gone to talk to her. It appears she's alive and well, which is a relief. The last thing we need is another dead body."

The woman looked like a deer about to bolt and if Krish didn't have her hair wrapped around a brush, she may have done. "Are you nearly finished?" she asked nervously.

"Almost, dear." He patted her on the shoulder.

"I wonder if she is the killer," Penny murmured, but luckily the nervous woman didn't hear. Daisy would have to have a word with the staff. It was one thing ferreting out information, but quite another frightening the customers—and it wouldn't get them any repeat business.

"Lilly wouldn't hurt a fly," blurted out a girl sitting at Asa's nail bar.

Daisy turned in surprise. She was young, probably the same age as Asa, with striking features and cornflower-blue hair. There was a piercing through her nose. Asa was painting her nails the same color as her hair. "Do you know her?" Daisy asked.

The blue head bobbed. "Yeah, I used to work with Tom. He was a right laugh, he was. Always kidding around. We used to call him Mr. Life of the Party."

"Really?" Daisy, brush in one hand, bowl of tint in the other, walked over to where the girl sat. "Where did you work with him?"

"Rising Star. It's a charity based in Esher."

"Yes, I know it," Daisy said. "What did you do for them, if you don't mind me asking?"

"I don't mind." She grinned in an easygoing manner. Daisy liked her immediately. "I was just an admin assistant, but Thomas, he was a VIP, a high roller. Everybody loved him."

Not everybody, Daisy thought.

The girl continued, "He donated thousands to the charity each month."

"Thousands?" Daisy wasn't aware that he and Hannah had been that well-off. Maybe the girl was exaggerating.

"Yeah, he was a big spender; that's why he was a VIP. He did a lot for the kids too. He coached football on Saturday mornings and he always volunteered to be Santa at the Christmas parties. He made a great one too." It was clear she'd been fond of him.

"Is that what he was doing on Christmas Eve, the night he disappeared?" Daisy asked, even though she'd heard this before from Lightman. It never hurt to get a second opinion.

"Yes, I remember that night well because it was so weird. Everybody was really worried about him when he didn't show up because it wasn't like Tom to let us down." She shook her head at the memory. "The poor kids were devastated. Bas—he's the owner—had to get an elf to hand out the presents. He wasn't nearly as good as Tom."

This description of Tom was similar to Lightman's. Perhaps he wasn't as bad as his wife had made him out to be. The impression she'd given was of an unfaithful husband who preferred the pub to the family home.

The girl pursed her lips. "I couldn't believe it when people said he'd done a runner. No way, not Tom. He wasn't like that. And all this time he'd been murdered, and that very night too." She shivered.

"That's creepy," Asa said, applying clear varnish over the cornflower-blue talons.

"Yeah, it totally freaked me out," agreed the girl. "But it makes sense. I knew he hadn't run off with Lilly. He wasn't like that and neither was she."

"You knew them both?" Daisy perched against a nearby basin.

"Yeah, the pub Lilly worked at was across the road from the charity's offices. It was our local. That's how Tom and Lilly met. She was a bundle of fun, that girl. Always joking and laughing. They made a good pair."

More interesting intel. Yvette had said she was always smiling too.

"Did Lilly know he was married?" Daisy asked.

"Sure, but he wasn't happy. I heard a rumor that he was going to leave his wife, but obviously that never happened."

"No, he didn't get the chance."

"Tragic," murmured the girl, then her expression changed as she admired her nails. "Awesome job, Asa. Thanks! These are going to go down a treat at the battle of the bands."

Daisy thanked her and, deep in thought, returned to her customer. Where had Thomas Pierce got that kind of money from? Was he into something illegal? Had he threatened to leave Hannah? Is that why she killed him?

Daisy thought about the crime scene, and how the victim had been lured there, then hit on the head with a hammer. How his body had been stuffed up inside the chimney. Was Hannah capable of that? Daisy frowned. As convenient as that theory was, Hannah just didn't fit the profile.

"Was that girl with the blue hair a friend of yours?" Daisy asked a bit later when they had a short lull in the stream of customers. She'd seen Asa hugging her when she'd left.

"Wendy? Yes, I've known her for years. We're not close, but we've been to some of the same gigs." Asa was very much into her live music, particularly reggae, and knew several of the local bands. "She used to go out with the drummer from Rock Steady, but they broke up this summer. He wanted to concentrate on his music, you know?"

Daisy blinked at her. She had no idea who Rock Steady was.

"Now she's dating Jack, from the Fox and Hound. They're much better suited."

"Is her phone number on the system?" Daisy asked, thinking McGuinness might like a word with her, but she didn't say as much to Asa, whose fear and distrust of the police ran deep.

"Yep, she's in there."

The whole afternoon, Daisy wondered whether McGuinness had managed to meet with Lilly Rosewood—now Westerford—and what he'd found out. She was also eager to tell him what she'd discovered about Thomas Pierce.

It was only when she was clearing up for the day, that her phone finally buzzed. Her heart leaped as the detective's name flashed across the screen. She turned down Miley Cyrus, who was rocking around the Christmas tree, and grabbed the phone.

"Paul? What did you discover?"

"Hello to you too, Daisy," he said dryly.

"Sorry, but I've been desperate to find out how you got on."

He chuckled. "Your enthusiasm is admirable. I met with Lilly Westerford. She is married and that's why she changed her name. She wasn't intentionally hiding from the police."

Daisy's head was filled with questions. "Did she say why she took off at the same time Thomas Pierce disappeared?"

"We had an interesting conversation," he began. Daisy could hear his car indicator flicking in the background, so she knew he was driving. She felt a pang of disappointment that he'd collected his car without dropping in to see her in person. It had only been parked at the end of the High Street.

"Yes, actually she did. Get this, she left Edgemead because Pierce broke it off with *her*. Apparently, he'd found out his wife was having an affair with his business partner and he was mad as hell. He told Lilly he was still in love with Hannah and was going to win her back."

"Really?" Now Daisy was really confused. "I heard a rumor that he was planning on leaving Hannah for Lilly."

"From who?" barked McGuinness.

"From this girl who came into the salon to get her nails done. She's a friend of Asa's. She worked with Thomas at Rising Star, and she knew Lilly because the Coach and Horses was their local. She said that's where Thomas met Lilly."

"Interesting. Well, someone's lying. Lilly claims she left town because she couldn't stand to see them together. She took it rather hard, from what I could gather."

"Maybe Thomas had been planning on leaving Hannah, but when he found out about her affair, he changed his mind. After all, they had a daughter together, and if there was ever a reason to try again, that was it."

"I suppose it's possible," McGuinness said, but he didn't sound convinced. "On the other hand, he could have snapped when he found out about his wife and Clive and attacked her. Maybe Hannah hit him in self-defense."

"With a hammer?"

McGuinness grunted.

"Or maybe it was Lilly?" Daisy mused. "She would have been desperate not to lose him."

"This is just guesswork," McGuinness said. "We don't have any evidence that proves either of them did it. It would really help if we could find the murder weapon."

Despite the thorough forensic search of Holly Lodge, the hammer used to strike Thomas Pierce hadn't been found.

"You could get a warrant to search their premises?" Daisy suggested.

"I considered it, except they've both moved since the murder. Hannah married Clive and they moved to Esher and Lilly's also married and is now living in south London. It's extremely unlikely we'll find anything two years down the line. I don't want to waste the department's resources for nothing. We're overstretched as it is."

Daisy had to admit he was probably right. Not only did he have to find out who the killer was, but he had to do it within the confines of the police budget and under the eyes of the police commissioner, the public prosecutor, and the press. That was a lot of people to answer to.

"Do either of them have alibis?" Daisy glanced out of the window. It had stopped snowing, but now the High Street had turned into a sludgy mess. Cars hooted as the traffic crawled down the road and pedestrians side-stepped puddles as they rushed about doing last-minute shopping. Above them, the Christmas streetlights twinkled merrily, oblivious to the chaos below.

McGuinness's voice faded as he drove through a bad reception area. Daisy strained to hear was he was saying. "Lilly doesn't. She was supposed to be working at the pub on Christmas Eve, but the manager said she didn't show up for her shift."

"What about Hannah?" Daisy tried to remember what the young mother had said.

"Nothing we can check," admitted McGuinness. "She insists she was home with the baby, but I do want to speak to her again to confirm Lilly's story about the break-up. With two different accounts, I have to find out the truth."

Daisy remembered something else Wendy had said. "Oh, while you're at it, you might want to ask her about the donations her husband made to the Rising Star charity. Apparently he gave thousands a month."

"Thousands?" repeated McGuinness.

That had been her reaction too. "Yes, according to Asa's friend, he was a big spender. She called him a high roller. I didn't think they had that kind of money."

"They didn't," said McGuinness thoughtfully. "At least not according to their bank statements. Thanks, Daisy, I'll certainly ask her about it."

"Do you think you'll be able to come to the Christmas market tomorrow afternoon?" Daisy asked before he ended the call.

There was a brief pause. "I think I can get away."

"Great. The whole town will be there." She tried not to sound too eager. "You might pick up some useful tidbits of information."

"Maybe." She could hear he was smiling. "I wouldn't mind talking to that friend of Asa's. Wendy, was it?"

"Yes. I'll ask Asa if she's going."

"Great. So I'll see you there?"

"Yes, see you there."

Chapter 12

"Now it's beginning to feel like Christmas," said Krish as Daisy locked the hairdressing salon's doors and they stepped out into the High Street. They didn't usually work on Sundays, but they'd been so busy, Daisy had agreed to see a few desperate customers in the morning and Krish had volunteered to help out. He lived above the newsagent a few blocks away and had insisted it wasn't a big deal to come in on his day off.

"Are you coming to the market?" Daisy asked.

He grinned. "You betcha! I'm meeting Douglas there."

"Douglas, eh?" Daisy raised an inquisitive eyebrow. Krish hadn't had an easy time of it growing up being both Indian and gay, but since he'd moved to Edgemead, he'd really settled in and was now one of her best friends. His boundless energy was infectious, the customers loved him, and he was an essential part of her team. He'd taken a bit of a knock earlier in the year when his partner had been stabbed right in front of him, so Daisy was glad he'd bounced back and was dating again.

"We first met at a yoga retreat in the summer, but nothing came of it, and then we bumped into each other at Fortnum's the other day. He lives in Richmond, which isn't far from here." Richmond was two stops away by train and also on the River Thames. It was a lovely town, bigger than Edgemead, and a lot more expensive being that much closer to London.

"He sounds great. I can't wait to meet him."

They strolled arm in arm down the High Street, admiring the festive decorations in the shop windows. Krish had an excellent eye for detail, and he'd told Daisy once that if he hadn't become a hairdresser, he'd probably have done something in the way of interior design. They crossed the road and turned down a narrow, cobbled alleyway to the village green where the Christmas market was being held. Festive music floated over the still, icy air toward them and it wasn't long before they heard the sound of laughter and of people enjoying themselves. They exited the alleyway and crossed the narrow lane to the green, which pulsed with activity. Stalls covered almost every square inch, and there were hundreds of people milling around, sampling the local produce and buying last-minute Christmas gifts. Kids ran amok, pursued by anxious parents terrified of losing them in the crowd, couples strolled arm in arm, and the smell of hamburgers and roasted chestnuts filled the air.

It didn't take Daisy long to locate Floria and Josh, who

were standing in front of a hot-chocolate stand. Krish hugged her goodbye and skipped off to find Douglas, while Daisy joined her friends.

"I'm so glad you could make it." Floria squeezed her hand. "I was worried you'd have to work."

"We closed early." She smiled at them. "I wouldn't miss this for the world."

"Hello, Daisy. Would you like a hot chocolate?" Josh asked over his shoulder. He'd been standing in the short queue. In front of him, a customer turned around with two hot chocolates laden with whipped cream and covered in sprinkles. Her mouth started watering.

"Ooh, yes, please. Those look divine."

"There you guys are," said Donna, coming up. Her cheeks were flushed from the cold and her dark, cloudy hair was loose and wild, framing her heart-shaped face. "Look who I found lurking at the chestnut stand."

Mimi came forward, her arm around one of the handsomest men Daisy had ever seen. His chiseled face was tanned by the Australian sun, and he had cobalt-blue eyes framed by criminally long lashes. Unlike Josh, who was dressed in jeans and a ski jacket, he wore a smart suit under a tailored, winter coat. Daisy did a double take. She'd been expecting a grungy, tattooed rocker-type, not this suave, handsome businessman, then she remembered he owned a hotel group.

"Meet my husband, Rob," Mimi said, beaming up at him. It was clear she adored him.

Daisy gave him a friendly hug. "Hi, Rob, I'm Daisy. It's a pleasure to finally meet you."

He hugged her back. "Ah, the sleuthing hairdresser. Mimi's told me a lot about you and your investigating prowess. I hear you put the local police to shame." He grinned and Daisy liked the mischievous twinkle in his eye.

She shook her head. "Oh, I wouldn't put it quite like that."

"Of course she does," Floria gushed. "The handsome detective McGuinness would be quite lost without her."

Donna laughed. "You do have a knack for this sort of thing, Daisy."

"I hear you're helping the police find out who murdered the man found at Holly Lodge?" Rob said.

"I'm trying to." Daisy grimaced. So far, they hadn't made much progress. They were no closer to discovering who the killer was than when they started. The investigation seemed to have gone in a full circle.

"Here's your handsome detective now," whispered Floria, as McGuinness marched up, his coat billowing out behind him. Daisy felt a flurry of butterflies in her stomach. He was always so imposing, which made him impossible to ignore. He matched Josh in the height department— and Josh was a giant who used to play professional rugby—and he was at least half a foot taller than the suave, suntanned Rob, who wasn't short by any stretch of the imagination. Daisy made the introductions and after McGuinness had shaken hands with Rob and eyed him up, he took Daisy aside.

"Hannah confirmed that on the day he died, Thomas Pierce confronted her about her relationship with Clive. They had an argument, but she denies it got violent. When he'd calmed down, they talked and he told her he was going to stop seeing Lilly. By then she'd fallen for Clive, but Thomas was adamant, so Hannah agreed to give it another go, for Elly's sake. Then that night, he went to the Christmas party and didn't come back."

"Lilly was telling the truth," Daisy whispered. "He did dump her."

"It appears so," he replied, eyeing her hot chocolate.

"Do you want one?" she offered with a smile. "It's delicious."

"I'll get it."

He ordered one without the whipped cream and sprinkles and then they strolled along the rows of stalls, browsing the sparkling display of Christmas gifts and crafts on offer. There were homemade toys, garden accessories, baked goods, jams and chutneys, and even gifts for pets. Mimi and Rob strolled along behind them, holding hands, while Floria and Josh brought up the rear. Donna had gone to meet her husband Greg, who was running late.

"Oh, that's Wendy, the girl who worked with Thomas Pierce at Rising Star." Daisy pointed the young woman with blue hair out to McGuinness. "That's Asa with her."

"Let's go and say hello," McGuinness suggested, changing direction. Daisy knew Asa wasn't going to like that and she was right. As soon as the nail technician saw them coming, she grabbed Wendy's arm and they disappeared into the crowd.

"Sorry, she's not a fan," Daisy explained with a wry smile.

"I remember." McGuinness frowned. "I wanted to have a word with her friend, though."

"Asa still hasn't forgiven you for interrogating her earlier this year."

"I was just doing my job." He glanced at Daisy, his gaze intense. "You've forgiven me, right?"

Daisy felt herself grow warm. "Of course I have," she said softly.

He held her gaze. "I don't know if I ever said as much, but I'm sorry I put you through that. I knew you had nothing to do with the crime, but . . ."

"It's okay." She swallowed. He was so close, she could smell his aftershave. The Christmas shoppers swirled around them but she was only aware of him. "I know you were just doing your job."

"I was, and I had to follow standard operating procedures. I couldn't be seen to show you any leniency because of our—our relationship."

"Our relationship?" she echoed quietly. This was the first time he'd acknowledged anything of the sort.

His voice dropped. "Whatever this is that's happening between us."

Daisy's heart hammered in her chest. She took a step closer toward him. His fingers intertwined with hers and his gaze dropped to her lips. She held her breath. Was he going to kiss her?

A voice penetrated their little bubble. "Detective Inspector McGuinness—just the man I wanted to talk to."

They both glanced up in surprise and Daisy took a hasty step backwards, unlinking their hands. The spell was broken. Clive Collington stood behind them, a beer in one hand and a hot dog in the other. "I was going to call you after Christmas, but I'm glad I've bumped into you. I've remembered something that I thought might help."

This wasn't really the place for an interview. A group of teenagers ran past, holding cotton candy and laughing, while a juggler performed for a gathering crowd.

"Let's go over there." McGuinness led Clive away from the growing throng of people to a quieter spot.

Daisy saw Floria watching them out of the corner of her eye. She waved and gave Daisy a thumbs-up.

"The other night, I was talking to Hannah about this ghastly business and how lucky I was that you managed to trace that bed-and-breakfast I stayed in." He chuckled. "Thank you for that. I was beginning to feel like your prime suspect."

"You were," grunted McGuinness, wiping the smile off Clive's face. Daisy wondered where this was going.

"That's when I remembered the phone call."

McGuinness's head shot up. "What phone call?"

Clive licked a drop of ketchup off his thumb. "From the person who wanted to view Holly Lodge."

"When exactly did this call take place?" McGuinness switched from annoyed to businesslike in an instant. His shoulders straightened and his head leaned forward as he focused all his attention on Clive. Daisy, still reeling from what had almost happened between them, was listening too.

"On Christmas Eve. I was on my way up to Yorkshire and had to put him on speaker in the car."

McGuinness glanced at Daisy and she knew what he was thinking. Could this mystery caller be their killer?

"Was it a man or a woman?" Daisy asked, coming forward.

Clive glanced at her in surprise, but he answered the question. "A man. He was interested in the property and wanted to arrange an urgent viewing. Of course, that was impossible since it was the twenty-fourth of December and I was halfway up the M1 motorway at the time, so I passed him on to Tom."

"You gave him Tom's number?" McGuinness repeated.

"Yes, he seemed surprised. I think he thought I was Tom."

"Did he give a name?" asked Daisy.

"If he did, I don't remember. It was two years ago. In fact, I'm surprised I remembered the phone call at all. It was only because I was telling my wife about the trip, that it came to me."

"Thank you very much, Clive," said Daisy. "That's extremely helpful." She nudged McGuinness in the side. He was still staring at Clive, lost in thought.

"Yes. Thanks for letting us know." Daisy knew his brain was working overtime, trying to figure out how they could check who the caller was.

"I've got Clive Collington's phone records back at the station," he said, as soon as the real estate agent had walked away. "But only his recent ones. I'm going to have to request the ones from two years ago to try and trace that call."

"What about Thomas's?" Daisy asked. "Do you have his? If that man called Thomas, he could have been the one to lure him to Holly Lodge."

"But why call Clive first?" said McGuinness. "It doesn't make sense. If he wanted to call Thomas, why not just do that directly?"

"Maybe he didn't have his number," said Daisy, frowning. "The call could have come through the office and diverted to Clive's phone. Maybe the caller thought he was speaking to Thomas. Clive did say the caller seemed surprised when he was passed on."

"It's possible." McGuinness glanced at his watch. Daisy sensed he wanted to rush off and check the phone logs.

"If you need to go . . ." she began.

He shook his head. "It's Sunday. I won't be able to get hold of the telephone operators today. It'll have to wait until tomorrow."

"Then, you may as well relax and enjoy yourself."

He grunted, then took her hand. "Daisy—"

Just then a piercing scream rang out and Asa bolted out of the crowd toward them. Her eyes were wild and she was shaking from head to toe. She gripped Daisy's arm, without even acknowledging the detective. "Oh, Daisy, you have to come quickly. Wendy's dead! She's been strangled."

Chapter 13

Daisy and McGuinness zigzagged around Christmas shoppers as they sped through the rows of stalls after Asa. They got to the end of a row and behind a green tent they spotted a slim young woman lying on the snowy ground, her blue hair spread out around her.

"It is her," whispered Daisy, bending down to see if she was still alive. A cord of some sort was twisted around her neck.

"Stay back," barked McGuinness.

Daisy took a few stumbling steps backwards. She'd forgotten about contaminating the crime scene. Her over-riding instinct had been to check if Wendy was still alive.

A crowd had started to gather around the body. "Everybody get back!" he bellowed, waving his arms. He knelt down to check for signs of life, but finding none, he shook his head. "I'm sorry."

Asa collapsed into Daisy's arms, sobbing loudly and everybody stared at each other, ashen-faced.

"She's been strangled by a string of Christmas lights." McGuinness studied the cord around her neck without touching it. The row of lights had been pulled off the back of the tent and used to throttle her. In the process, the plug had been yanked out of the generator, disconnecting them.

Daisy stared at the body of the striking young girl who only yesterday had been sitting, so full of life, in her salon. Her gaze fell on her perfectly groomed blue nails and tears welled up in her eyes. She blinked them back. If Asa hadn't been sobbing in her arms, she may well have given in to the tears herself.

"There's a bruise on her face," said McGuinness, peering in. "It looks like she's been hit. It could have been administered by her attacker, but I don't think it's that recent. I'd say this is a day old, at least."

"She didn't have a bruise when she came into the salon," Daisy remarked. "I'd have noticed."

"Well, someone hit her." McGuinness got to his feet.

"What can I do?" Daisy whispered. She felt numb. How could this have happened? And right here at the Christmas fete?

"Nothing. We have to preserve the crime scene until forensics gets here." He turned to face the crowd and raised his voice. "Did anyone see anything? If you did, please come forward."

Several heads shook and people started backing away. McGuinness focused on the crowd, and Daisy knew he was looking for anyone acting suspiciously. Murderers often returned to the scene of the crime. She too scanned the onlookers, but didn't find anything untoward. Most of them just looked shocked, a feeling she could relate to.

A uniformed police officer came forward. McGuinness took him aside and told him what had happened and requested he call for backup so they could cordon off the area and preserve the crime scene. The policeman wasted no time in pulling out his radio and contacting dispatch.

"Asa, were you with Wendy when this happened?" He turned back to the nail technician, still clutching onto Daisy.

She sniffed and shook her head. "N—no, sir. I went to get us a drink and when I got back, I found her like this."

"Where did you leave her?" Daisy asked gently.

"In front of this stall." Asa pointed to the green tent behind them. "I was only gone a minute."

"It takes at least three to strangle someone," McGuinness said.

Daisy shot him a warning look. Asa was distraught enough already; she didn't need the detective criticizing her every word. He softened his tone. "Okay, so did she say anything before you left her? Was she agitated or upset?"

Asa wiped her eyes and tried to think. "No, she was normal."

"Are you sure?"

"Yeah, I'm sure." Then she stopped and frowned. "But she said something strange."

"What was it?" Daisy asked.

"About half an hour ago she spotted someone in the crowd. It was odd because she stopped suddenly and stared at them, then she said, 'I remember now.'"

"Who was it?" McGuinness snapped.

"Remembered what?" asked Daisy at the same time.

"I don't know," Asa cried. "I wasn't paying attention. I thought it was some random person that she knew."

"Please, try to think," Daisy pressed. "This person may have been the one who killed her."

Asa's lip quivered and she buried her head into Daisy's shoulder. "I'm sorry, I can't," came the muffled response.

"Was it a man or a woman?" Daisy pressed, putting an arm around her. She could feel Asa trembling. McGuinness gazed at Asa's head, his eyes burning. Daisy shared his frustration.

"She didn't say." And she broke into a fresh flood of tears.

"We won't get anything out of her now," Daisy told him, stroking Asa's back. "She's too traumatized."

Krish had come to see what all the commotion was about and stood a few meters away with his new beau. Daisy beckoned to him and he rushed over. "Who is it? Anyone we know?"

"Unfortunately, yes. It's Wendy, Asa's friend." Asa clung onto her, afraid to let go.

"Oh, no!" Krish exclaimed. "What happened?"

"She was strangled," Daisy told him. She didn't mention the Christmas lights.

"Bloody hell." He glanced Asa. "Is she all right?"

Daisy shook her head. "No, she's in a bit of a state. Would you mind looking after her?"

Krish immediately put his arm around the sobbing Asa.

"Thanks, Krish." Daisy extricated herself, then squeezed Asa's hand. "Krish is going to make sure you get home safely, and I'll call later to check on you." Hopefully she'd remember something more once the initial shock wore off.

"Okay." Asa sniffed and glanced once more at Wendy's body. "I can't believe she's gone. One minute we were laughing and joking, and the next . . ." She sniffed. "It happened so fast."

"Krish?" Daisy warned, sensing Asa was seconds away from a full-blown meltdown.

He led her away from the crime scene. "Come on, babe. Let's get you home."

As they left, the CSI van arrived, ramping the pavement and pulling up on the grass beside the tent. White-clad forensic officers piled out, carrying an assortment of equipment. Within minutes, they'd erected a tent over Wendy's body to protect her from prying eyes and the elements.

While this was happening, McGuinness had a brief chat with the lead pathologist, who then disappeared into the tent, eager to get to work. Every minute counted when gathering evidence. A police unit arrived and set up a perimeter around the crime scene to keep the crowds back.

"Christmas lights?" Daisy mused, once McGuinness had rejoined her. The crowd had been dispersed and Daisy could hear the festivities continuing like nothing had happened.

"Yes, strange choice of weapon," he muttered. "I can't say I've ever seen that before."

"Impulsive," Daisy remarked. "The killer grabbed whatever he could get hold of in the heat of the moment. I don't think this was planned."

"Are we assuming it's a he now?" McGuinness said.

"He or she," Daisy corrected. "Although, I'm standing by my theory that it was a man."

"I don't believe in coincidences." His eyes were hard as he looked at Daisy. "The person Wendy saw must have recognized her too and jumped at the first opportunity to get her alone. He must have coerced her back here, grabbed the cord of lights off the back of the tent, and used them to strangle her."

Daisy agreed that was the most probable scenario.

"I can't believe there's a market full of people here, but nobody saw a thing." Daisy glanced around at the crowds, but they were all in front of the tent, browsing the market stalls, not behind it. "I suppose no one had any reason to come back here. There's nothing here except the electricity generator."

"Agreed," said McGuinness. "And the road is lined with thick oak trees, so visibility from the street would have been limited if someone had been walking or driving by. We'll appeal for witnesses, anyway, just in case. I'll get the uniform division onto it."

He strode off to talk to the officers from Edgemead police station.

Daisy questioned the distraught owner of the stall inside the tent that sold hot dogs, hamburgers, coffees, pastries, and cold drinks. "Did you hear anything or notice anything unusual in the last half hour?"

He gawked at the illuminated tent where the pathologist was analyzing the body and forensic officers were processing the crime scene. "Is there really a dead body in there?"

"I'm afraid so," Daisy replied. "Could you answer my question?"

He shook his head, as if in a dream. "No, not a thing, but it's hard to hear anything over the coffee machine and customers."

Daisy couldn't argue with him about that. She'd been inside the tent and could testify that hearing anything out back beyond the generator was unlikely.

"You didn't see anyone walk around the back?"

"I wouldn't have noticed." He wiped a hand across his brow. "I'm busy grilling sausages and serving customers, not studying the passersby."

"Okay, thanks." Daisy took his contact details down just in case McGuinness or Sergeant Buckley wanted to interview him again, and then went to find Floria and the others, who were lingering behind the police cordon, talking in somber tones.

"Daisy, did you know her?" Floria asked as soon as she joined them.

"Sort of." Daisy couldn't suppress a sad little sigh. "She came into the salon yesterday to have her nails done. She was a friend of Asa's."

"Poor thing," murmured Donna. "We saw Krish lead her off. She wasn't in a good way."

"No, she's pretty upset, but Krish will make sure she's okay. She lives with her aunt and uncle, so they'll take care of her."

"Was this connected to the murder at Holly Lodge?" Mimi asked. Her husband Rob looked on worriedly. He was probably wondering what on earth they'd got themselves into.

"We're not sure yet, but it could be." She was almost certain that it was, but until they had proof, they shouldn't conjecture. Not that it would do much good. News of the murder had spread like wildfire among the crowd and the buzzing, festive atmosphere had dialed down a notch. There was less laugher, more furtive glances toward the cordon, and a general sense of unease. Daisy noticed several television vans pull up beyond the oak trees. "Here we go," she murmured, nodding toward them.

Josh scowled. "They don't waste any time, do they? McGuinness will send them packing." He was right. The gruff detective strode toward them, his shoulders tense, a stormy expression on his face. By the wagging of his finger and the aggressive stance of his body, Daisy could imagine what he was saying to them. Sure enough, a short time later, the police had extended the cordon right back to the road and the press were left to film from afar, their lenses poking through the snow-covered branches of the trees.

"That's my cue to leave." Mimi took her husband's arm. "You know what the press are like." A celebrity caught in the vicinity of a crime scene was always big news.

"I think we'll go too." Donna flashed them an apologetic look. "I've got a recital on Boxing Day at the Royal Star and Garter and I need to practice. Will you guys be okay?"

"I'll make sure they get home safely." Josh shook Greg's hand and gave Donna a hug. "Talk to you later."

"What now?" Floria gazed past Daisy to the forensic tent where officers were carrying the sheathed body out to a waiting ambulance. They fell silent and watched. The covered figure seemed absurdly small and slender underneath the black plastic. Once again, Daisy was hit by a wave of sadness. How had this happened? What link did

Wendy have to the murderer? She watched until they'd lifted the body inside and shut the ambulance doors. Whatever it was, she vowed, she was going to find out.

"I'm sorry, guys," she said to them. "I need to go home, take a hot bath, and try to make sense of all this."

"Shouldn't you leave it to the police?" said Josh, concerned. "If this is the same culprit, he's already murdered two people."

"He's right, Dais." Floria's normally smooth forehead creased with worry. "It's obvious he'll stop at nothing to make sure his identity stays secret."

"That's why we've got to stop him," Daisy argued.

"I'm not so sure McGuinness would agree to you being so involved," Josh pointed out.

Floria nudged him. "Here he comes now."

McGuinness stalked toward them, his expression dour. "Daisy, can I borrow you for a second?"

Floria shot her husband a triumphant look. "See, she's vital to the police investigation."

Josh spread his arms in a gesture of defeat, but Daisy could see the concern in his eyes. "I'll be careful, Josh. I promise."

He gave her a nod. "Call me if you need me."

"Daisy?" McGuinness pointed to the ambulance where a tall Rastafarian was standing. By his mannerisms, he was extremely upset and agitated. He paced up and down, stamped his feet and flung his dreadlocked mane out of his face.

"I'm coming."

She waved goodbye to Floria and Josh and followed McGuinness across the frosty lawn.

"Wendy's boyfriend just arrived," he said under his

breath. "Could you talk to him and find out if he' and Wendy had had a fight recently?"

Daisy cottoned on to his line of thinking. "You think he might have been the one who hit her?"

"That's what I want to find out. If he did, we can't rule out the possibility that he might have strangled her too."

Daisy gave a sharp intake of breath. "In which case, this might not be connected to Thomas Pierce's murder."

"We have to investigate all possibilities," he said tersely.

"Why do you want me to do this?" Daisy asked. "Surely you or one of the police officers here would be more qualified?"

"There are no female officers on duty, I've checked. You have a soft way about you," he said. "He might be more willing to open up to you about the fight. I'll follow up with him in a bit. Don't let him leave until I've spoken to him, okay?"

Daisy felt a surge of pride. McGuinness needed her and trusted her enough to play an active role in this investigation. "Where's Sergeant Buckley?" she asked. This would normally be his job.

"He's gone to his family in Manchester for Christmas," McGuinness said in a dry voice. "I stupidly gave him the holidays off."

That explained his absence since he'd driven to Yorkshire to interview Clive Collington's mother. He must have gone straight to Manchester afterwards, since it wasn't far from where Clive's mother lived in the care home. "I'll take care of the boyfriend," she said with a smile.

He put a hand on her arm. "Thanks, Daisy."

The pathologist came over. "We found some skin underneath the victim's fingernails. It looks like she tried to fend off her attacker."

"That's good news," McGuinness said. "We might be able to identify him, then."

Daisy felt a surge of hope for the first time since she'd seen Wendy's body. If the killer's DNA was in the system, they'd have their man.

Chapter 14

Daisy took Wendy's boyfriend, a trendily dressed Rastafarian who said his name was Bob, to the side. Forensic officers were traipsing to and from the tent to the van and there was still a crowd of onlookers peering over the police cordon, intrigued by what had happened.

"I'm very sorry for your loss," she said.

"Where's Wendy? That policeman said she was dead. Is that true?" His words ran into each other in his haste to get them out. It was clear the news he'd been given was taking a while to sink in.

"Yes, I'm afraid it's true. I'm sorry, Bob."

"Oh, God." He swayed dangerously. Daisy put her hand on his arm.

"Come on, let's sit down." There was a bench a few

meters away, under the oak trees. Daisy led Wendy's boyfriend toward it, then held his arm as he collapsed onto it. "How—how did this happen? I saw her a couple of hours ago." He stared up at Daisy with a dazed expression and she noticed his pupils were dilated. There was also a strong herbal smell on his clothing, which made her suspect he might not be in full control of his senses.

Perhaps that was a good thing, as his guard would be down, but it also made it less likely that he'd been able to murder his girlfriend. Wendy's killer had been able to think on his feet. He'd seized the opportunity to strangle his victim when no one was looking and used whatever was on hand to do it. Would Bob have had that kind of foresight?

He was rocking back and forth on the bench, twiddling his hands in front of him.

"When last did you see Wendy?" she asked him.

He didn't respond, so she repeated the question, placing her hand on his shoulder. He turned his unfocused eyes onto her. "I don't know, around twelvish," he said. "We met for lunch in the High Street and then she came here with Asa and I went to the pub with my mates. We're performing tonight at the Fox and Hound." If he could play a musical instrument in this state, he might be able to murder someone.

"Where are your mates now?" she asked him, thinking that if she could verify his alibi, there'd be no need for McGuinness to speak to him.

"They're still at the pub." He glanced at the forensic tent that was illuminated from the inside by some sort of portable forensic lamp. "Why can't I see her?"

"Because they need to make sure any evidence on or

around her body is preserved," Daisy explained. "The pathologist is with her now. Don't worry, he'll take good care of her."

"But what if it's not her?" His eyes kept darting to the tent and back at Daisy. "It might be a mistake. I need to make sure."

"It *is* her, Bob," Daisy said calmly. "I met her the other day at my hair salon and I've identified the body. So has Asa. I'm so sorry, but there is no doubt."

He dropped his head into his hands and sobbed, his shoulders shaking. Daisy patted him on the back. She felt for him, for all of Wendy's friends and family. Wendy was too young to die, especially in this horrible manner. Not that there was ever a good way to go. But strangled a week before Christmas . . . She shivered and tried not to think about it.

Bob sniffed and flung his dreadlocks back in an attempt to get control of himself. His face was wet with tears. He wasn't putting it on.

"Bob, can I ask if you and Wendy had a fight recently?"

"A fight?"

"Yes, I noticed she had a bruise on her face."

"Oh, that." He looked sheepish.

"How did it happen?" she asked gently.

"It was nothing. We had a row, but I didn't hit her. Not on purpose. I was waving my guitar around and she walked into it. It was an accident."

Daisy had no way of refuting that. "How did you know to come here?" she asked suddenly. If he'd been at the pub with his mates, how could he have known Wendy had been attacked?

He wiped his nose on the back of his sleeve. He had

two long fingernails on his right hand, typical of someone who played the guitar. "Ellis ran into the pub and told me something had happened on the green. He told me he'd seen a woman with blue hair surrounded by police, so I thought I'd better check it out. I still can't believe it's her."

"Ellis?"

"He's the guy that busks outside Tesco. He was walking past when he saw the police arrive."

"Ah." Daisy knew who he was talking about. She'd often seen the big black man playing his saxophone outside the supermarket. He was very good. Sometimes she even stopped to listen for a while, tossing a pound into his hat to show her appreciation.

Still, Bob had no alibi. "Let me walk you back to the Fox and Hound," she volunteered, getting to her feet. Her backside was cold and damp from the snow on the bench. He looked like he might refuse, but then he let her lead him away.

The Fox and Hound was a vibey, local pub situated at the top of the High Street. They served decent, English pub food and had live music on the weekends. It was packed with the lunchtime crowd, but in the corner, Daisy could see a group of guys that looked like they might be part of Bob's band. There was another man with dreadlocks, a tall, grungy-looking bloke with long hair, and a bald guy dressed in a leather jacket. Sure enough, Bob walked straight over to them.

"It *was* Wendy," he blurted out. "She's dead."

The looks on their faces varied from astonishment to uncertainty—was he kidding?—and then incredulity as they realized he was serious.

"No way!"

"For real?"

"What?"

Daisy held up her hand. "I'm afraid it's true," she said. "Bob's had a terrible shock. Maybe if one of you could see that he gets home? He's going to need some time to get over this."

It was the bald guy who said, "I'll take him home. My car's out back."

Bob shook his head. "Nah, I'm fine. We've got a gig to prepare for. Lloyd, grab me a beer, mate."

The band members looked at Daisy as if to ask permission for Bob's request. She bit her lip. "I'm not sure you should be drinking right now," she told him. "Wouldn't it be better if you went home?"

He shrugged. "I don't wanna be alone right now. This is the best place for me."

"It's okay," the long-haired guy said. "We'll keep an eye on him."

Lloyd moved off to the bar. Daisy hesitated. These guys didn't look like they were the most responsible people she'd ever met, but what could she do? If Bob wanted to stay and drown his sorrows, who was she to argue? He was a grown man. "Um, okay."

She turned away, but instead of leaving, she went to the bar. "Excuse me," she said to the bald guy who Bob had called Lloyd.

He turned around. "You staying for a pint?"

"No, thanks. I just wanted to confirm that Bob has been with you for the last few hours."

"Yeah, we met here after lunch and the only time he left was when Ellis ran in about twenty minutes ago. Why?" He frowned, his eyes narrowing. "Are you a copper?"

"No, I'm not." She backed away. It was time to go.

McGuinness would be wondering where she was. She zigzagged around the tables and pushed open the door. Once outside, she took a deep, steadying breath. Bob was in the clear.

Why target Wendy? Daisy dwelled on this as she walked down the cobbled path toward the green. She was so young, so innocent. There was only one explanation. Wendy must have recognized the killer in the crowd, and they had recognized her too. Paranoid that Wendy could identify them, they'd lured her to a private spot behind the tent and strangled her, using whatever was on hand. It had been an impulsive crime, driven by panic. The big question was who had Wendy seen? And was he still here?

McGuinness was waiting for her at the crime scene. "Where's Bob?" he asked. "I told you to keep him here."

"I went to check out his alibi," she replied. "He said he'd been with friends at the Fox and Hound, so I walked him back there to check it out. I thought it would save you having to do it later."

He gave her a hard look. "Daisy, why don't you ever listen to me? I still have to question them and document their names and addresses for the case file. A murder investigation is not just about proving who did it, it's also about proving who didn't. I need to corroborate Bob's alibi in court to show he's officially been ruled out as a suspect, else I might be seen as not doing my job properly."

Daisy closed her eyes. She'd messed up. "I'm sorry, I was trying to help."

He raked a hand through his hair. "I know, but you can't go about taking matters into your own hands. There are protocols to follow, which means you have to listen to what I say if you want any part in this investigation."

Daisy flushed. "Paul, I really am sorry."

He didn't look at her. "It's okay. We can still fix this. Is Bob still at the pub?"

She nodded miserably. "He didn't want to go home. They've got a gig tonight."

"He's playing tonight?" His eyebrows shot up.

"That's what he said. I wasn't sure it was a good idea, but he was adamant."

"Well, it's probably a good thing." He beckoned to a uniformed police officer. The man came right over. "Constable, could you go to the Fox and Hound and get the names and addresses of the guys who vouched for Bob, the victim's boyfriend? Daisy will show you who they are. If you could also corroborate what they told Daisy? I need it in writing."

He gave a curt nod. "Yes, sir." He knew the correct procedure to follow.

Daisy bit her lip. "I feel awful. I can't believe I didn't think of that." What Paul said made perfect sense. It seemed obvious now, but at the time, she'd thought it meant McGuinness could rule Bob out of his inquiries. She'd blatantly disregarded his instructions and ignored his years of experience, and now he'd never trust her at a crime scene again.

"That's okay, Daisy. I appreciate what you were trying to do." A scene-of-crime officer gestured to him. "Look, I've got to go. I'll speak to you soon, okay?"

"Okay."

The policeman looked at her expectantly. "Which way to the pub?"

Chapter 15

"Asa, what are you doing here?" Daisy asked as Asa walked into the hairdressing salon at eight-thirty on Monday morning.

"Working." The Afro-Caribbean girl sashayed past her to the nail bar, but Daisy could tell it was false bravado. "I can't let my customers down. There are only a few days to go before Christmas. Besides, what were you going to tell them?"

"I was going to cancel your appointments until after Christmas," she replied, but with everything going on, she hadn't got around to it yet. She still felt wretched about what had happened yesterday with Bob, and how she'd almost ruined the investigation. From now on, she was going to stay out of police business. No more taking matters into her own hands.

"Don't be ridiculous." Asa took off her jacket. "You can't turn all that business away."

Daisy hesitated. Asa looked fine, but then she was wearing makeup, which would hide her pallor. "Only if you're sure. You've had a terrible shock."

"I'm fine," Asa snapped, then her face fell. "It was a shock, but I know you and that scary detective will find whoever killed—whoever did that to Wendy. Besides, I need to keep busy." She hung her jacket on the coatrack and turned around. "Please, I can't be at home right now."

Daisy gave a sympathetic nod. She understood the need to keep active and they did have a long list of customers to get through today. The nail bar had become a popular feature and the revenue it was bringing in was substantial. "Okay," she relented, "but next year, we should think about getting you an assistant."

Asa managed a weak smile, but her face didn't light up like it normally did. "Thanks, Daisy."

"And if you need to go home or you feel like you're not coping, just let me know, okay?" Asa nodded and began to set up her workstation.

Krish breezed in soon after Asa, juggling four take-away cups from Starbucks. The coffee shop was only a few doors down from his apartment. "Gingerbread lattes, anyone?"

"Yes, please!" Penny, who was always in early, grabbed one from his hands before he'd even had a chance to take off his coat.

"Here, let me hold those for you," Daisy offered, taking them from him. He shuffled out of his coat and brushed a hand through his hair, which was glossy and thick, and styled in a devil-may-car manner. His maroon shirt had a starched collar and was shot through with silver thread that looked good against his olive skin. He always dressed well, but today he'd pulled out all the stops.

"Going somewhere nice?" Daisy asked, raising an eyebrow.

"How did you guess?" He grinned at her. "I'm meeting Douglas after work in Soho. We're going to a Christmas party at Sloane's." Sloane's, as far as Daisy could make out, was an über-trendy gay club in London's party district.

"All right for some," mumbled Asa from the corner. "My aunt and uncle are having a small get-together tonight, which usually means the whole neighborhood's invited." Asa was prone to exaggeration, but Daisy was pleased she would be surrounded by friends and family. It was the best thing for her, right now.

Krish handed her a latte. "I know you love it, Asa. You can't fool me." With a sheepish grin she accepted the coffee.

Daisy was dying to quiz her about yesterday. Had she remembered anything more about who Wendy had seen or what she'd said before she died? Except now wasn't the right time. She'd let Asa settle in first, and later they'd have another chat.

A knock on the door made her look up. Their first three appointments were waiting, as well as numerous other regulars and a few not-so regulars, all wanting an update on the murder at the Christmas market.

Daisy glanced at Krish. "You can do the honors."

"Sure thing." He took a deep breath and opened the door.

*   *   *

It was lunchtime before Daisy had an opportunity to speak to Asa in private. While the nail technician was having a break, she suggested they grab some sandwiches for the rest of the team. The High Street was bustling with Christmas shoppers, and they wove their way through the crowd to the supermarket. "I'm glad you're feeling better," Daisy told Asa, as they piled numerous chicken-and-mayo sandwiches into a basket.

"I'm trying not to think about it," she replied, tossing in several packets of crisps.

"I understand," said Daisy. That was a good short-term solution, but eventually, she'd have to come to terms with what had happened. "Asa, can I ask if you've remembered anything else about what Wendy said at the market when she saw that person she recognized?"

They'd wandered into the cool-drink aisle and it was freezing. Asa selected several cans of soda and put them into the basket along with the rest of the stuff.

"Asa?" Daisy prompted.

She refused to look at Daisy and stuck out her lower lip.

"If you've remembered something, you must tell me. It could help us find out who killed Wendy."

"But you'll go straight to 'im," she insisted. *'Im* was obviously DCI McGuinness.

"Yes, if it's got something to do with who murdered Wendy, I have to." She took a deep breath. "Don't you want to find out who killed her?"

Asa wrapped her arms around her middle to keep warm and stared at the floor. "Yeah, I guess so. It won't bring her back, though."

"No, it won't do that," Daisy agreed softly. "But at

least we can get justice for her, and for the man who died at Holy Lodge."

"Will it mean Mimi can move back into her house sooner?" Asa asked, glancing up.

"Yes, that too."

"Okay, then I'll tell you."

Daisy breathed a sigh of relief.

"Last night I thought really hard about what Wendy said when she saw the person in the crowd. Then it came to me."

"Yes?" Daisy leaned forward expectantly.

"She said she remembered whoever it was from the charity, with Tom."

Daisy frowned. "Do you remember her exact words?"

"Yeah. She saw the person in the crowd and stopped so suddenly I bumped into her. She frowned and said, *I remember now*. When I asked what she remembered, she said *From the charity, with Tom*. That was it. Then we went to get a hot dog."

Daisy's brain was working overtime, trying to put everything into perspective. "And this happened just before she was killed?"

Asa stared at the items in her basket. "I left her in the queue while I popped over to Sadie's stall for some mulled wine, and when I got back, she was lying there with those lights around her neck." Her lip quivered, but she didn't cry.

Daisy thought back. Wendy hadn't had the hot dogs in her hand when she'd been attacked, which meant the killer had enticed her behind the awning while she'd been standing in the queue. He certainly hadn't wasted any time.

They paid for the food and drink and headed back to the salon. "Are you going to call 'im, the scary detective?" Asa asked as they went inside into the warmth.

Daisy managed not to smile at that description. "Yes, but don't worry. If he needs to speak to you, I'll make sure I'm there. I won't leave you alone with him." After yesterday, Daisy knew McGuinness would want a record of every bit of information regarding Wendy's murder, including Asa's statement. If she'd learned anything, it was how important procedure was in ensuring a conviction.

Asa pulled a face. "Okay, thanks Daisy."

"Is Asa certain that's what Wendy said?" McGuinness bellowed down the line.

Daisy, who was sweeping up the hair on the floor, the phone balanced between her ear and her shoulder, cringed. "Yes, and you don't have to shout. I can hear you just fine."

"Sorry, occupational hazard."

Krish had left early, eager to get to his party in the West End, followed by Penny and Bianca, the trainee. Asa was in the kitchen washing up. Daisy didn't mind cleaning the salon. She enjoyed this time to herself. It helped her unwind.

"Yes, she's sure. Do you want me to bring her in to give an official statement?"

"That would be great, Daisy. You don't have to come out here, you can go to your local police station and do it. They'll forward me a copy."

"Okay, no problem." Daisy was keen to make up for her mistake yesterday. She wanted to show McGuinness that she was responsible and could be trusted at a crime scene.

"Do you think it could have been Bas Lightman?" McGuinness asked, after a brief pause.

"I doubt it," Daisy replied. "Wendy knew him well, since he used to be her boss. It's more likely to be someone connected with the charity who she hadn't seen for a while."

McGuinness grunted in agreement. "I'll get a list of names from Lightman. We need to check anyone connected with that charity—old employees, ex-donors, everyone."

"Look for people who don't live in the immediate area," suggested Daisy. "Wendy was obviously surprised to see them."

"Good point." She heard him scribbling on a piece of paper and imagined him sitting at his desk. She wondered what his work space was like, whether he was messy or organized. She'd bet on somewhere down the middle. Lots of paperwork, but organized in piles, a notepad brimming with tasks and details, but crossed out as he accomplished each one.

"She didn't specify whether it was male or female?" McGuinness asked.

"Unfortunately not." Daisy had wondered the same thing. "Do you think a woman could have strangled Wendy in that fashion?"

"Hmm . . . There would need to be a degree of strength involved, so it's more likely to be a man, but you never know. Wendy wasn't very big, so a strong woman could have come up behind her and surprised her."

"Yes, I suppose so," mused Daisy.

"And we're looking into the charity's accounts,"

McGuinness told her. Daisy heard shouting in the background.

"What's going on?"

"What? Oh, that. Nothing, just an uncooperative witness. It's the silly season. It brings out the worst in people."

"You were saying?"

"Yeah, his accounts. Our forensic accountant discovered some discrepancies in the donor records."

"Oh really?" Suddenly, Daisy was all ears.

"It appears that Thomas Pierce was a VIP donor. He donated ten thousand pounds to the charity on a monthly basis."

"Ten thousand pounds," Daisy croaked. "That's a lot of money to give away every month."

"Indeed. We're digging deeper. There was definitely something suspicious going on. Nobody donates that much to charity on a regular basis, not unless they're up to something."

"Okay, will you keep me posted?"

There was a pause, then he said, "Will do, and thanks for taking Asa to give her statement. That's really useful."

"You're welcome."

There was more yelling in the background. "I'd better go." His voice was strained. Daisy knew that for him, with two murder investigations on the go, it was going to be a long night.

Daisy had just left the local police station with a very grumpy Asa when her phone buzzed. She burrowed in her bag to find it. It was Floria.

"Darling, Mimi and I are about to head to Nonna

Lina's for an impromptu sups. The boys are watching football on TV. Can you join us?"

"That sounds great. I'll meet you there." Daisy immediately perked up. She said goodbye to Asa, who headed for the station, then walked up the High Street toward the restaurant, enjoying the Christmas music pouring out of the pubs and bars. She took a deep breath of snowy air and tried to shake off her somber mood. A night out with friends was just what she needed. Too much murder and mayhem was not good for the soul. She didn't know how McGuinness did it day in and day out.

Since Daisy was already in the vicinity, she got to the quaint Italian restaurant ahead of the others. Her spirits rose even more when she saw the twinkling Christmas tree through the glass frontage.

"Buonasera, signorina," gushed Cristiano as Daisy pushed open the door. Immediately, she was swamped with the delectable aroma of garlic and baking pizza dough. Her stomach rumbled.

"Buonasera, Cristiano, I'm meeting two girlfriends here. Do you have a table for us?" They hadn't made a reservation and by the looks of things, the little restaurant was quite full. The Christmas decorations gave the place a festive air. There was tinsel around the bar and over the framed Napoli street scenes on the walls. In the corner, by the window stood a glittering Christmas tree covered in multicolored lights. Italian opera was playing softly in the background.

"For you, we always have room." He grinned and led her to a small table at the back, discreetly removing the *reserved* sign. Daisy was a regular at Nonna Lina's and after going there at least once a month for the last five years, she knew the family fairly well. Guido, Cristiano's older brother, was the chef, while his mother was the manager. Occasionally, when they were busy, his wife helped wait tables. The restaurant had originally been opened by his grandmother, Lina, but she'd retired now—hence the name.

"Thank you, Cristiano, you're a star."

He beamed. "Your usual, signorina?"

"Yes, please. And three glasses."

He disappeared to fetch the wine. Daisy stretched her neck and felt the tension dissolve from her shoulders. The soft chattering of voices and the clinking of cutlery soothed her. While she waited for Floria and Mimi to arrive, she leaned back and observed the other clientele. Most of them were couples, eating and talking, their heads close together. Christmas was such a romantic time of year. She thought about Paul, and a pang of loneliness clutched at her heart. Would they ever get it together, or had she ruined it by breaking his trust? Ever since Wendy's death it had been back to business as usual. The truth was, he was far too busy for a relationship.

Daisy took a deep breath. Oh, well, she didn't need a man to be happy. She had her salon, her friends, and her little cottage, which was her sanctuary. Life was good.

There was a loud clatter as a man stood up and knocked his chair backwards. Daisy stared at him. It was Bas Lightman, she was sure of it. He was standing up, facing another man with a long, narrow face and a goatee. The wine bottle between them was empty and judging by the state of Lightman, he'd consumed most of it.

"I'm going to have to give it all bloody back, aren't I?" he was saying, his voice inordinately loud. Cristiano rushed over, concerned.

"Are you okay, Mr. Lightman? Can I get you a coffee?"

"I don't want a coffee," he stated, wobbling precariously. "I'd like a bottle of scotch, if you must know."

"Come on, Bas," said his friend, standing up. "Let's go. The check please, Cristiano."

Cristiano rushed to oblige. The two men had drawn the attention of most of the restaurant.

"I don't have it," he was saying in his booming voice. "It's gone."

Luckily, everyone's attention was diverted by Mimi and Floria arriving.

"That's Mimi Turner," whispered the woman next to Daisy to her husband, who looked up, confused.

"Who?"

"You know, the famous pop star!"

Daisy grinned and waved. The two women made their way through the restaurant, drawing stares and whispers as they went. Floria was the queen of style in a faux fur coat with knee-high boots, her blond hair a mass of waves around her smiling, heart-shaped face, while Mimi looked every inch the pop star in studded boots over tight black leather trousers and a fur-lined leather jacket.

Cristiano sighed in relief as he managed to get Bas Lightman and his partner out of the restaurant with minimal fuss. Before Lightman left, however, Daisy overheard him saying to Mr. Goatee, "The fraudulent bastard's going to bankrupt me. I knew it was a bad idea taking him on." She wondered if he was referring to Thomas Pierce.

Chapter 16

"Do you know what time it is?" McGuinness grumbled into the phone.

"I know you're still at the office," Daisy retorted.

There was a stony silence, then a sigh. "What can I do for you, Daisy?"

"It's more what I can do for you," she replied. "I had dinner at Nonna Lina's tonight and guess who was there?"

McGuinness sounded tired. "I don't know. Surprise me."

"Bas Lightman."

"Really?" His voice perked up. "What was he doing in Edgemead?"

"Nonna Lina's is a really good restaurant," Daisy said. "It's not unfeasible that someone would travel from Esher to dine there."

"Okay, so he ate there. What's unusual about that?"

"It's what he said *while* he was there that was interesting," she explained. "And by the way, he wasn't in a good state. I'd say he'd polished off most of a bottle of Merlot and was demanding whiskey when his friend escorted him out."

"We're looking into the charity's accounts," McGuinness explained. "Maybe that's what has him rattled."

"That's precisely what it is," Daisy told him. "He said—and I quote—*that fraudulent bastard is going to bankrupt me. I knew it was a mistake taking him on.*"

There was a pause, then McGuinness said, "Was he referring to Thomas Pierce?"

"I believe so," said Daisy. "Who else could he have meant? You did say there were discrepancies in the donor records, right?"

"Yes, we think Thomas Pierce was using the charity to launder money."

"Launder?" Daisy whispered. She had waited until she got home before she'd called Paul. Even though it was nearly midnight, she knew he'd still be working the case. Once he got his hooks into something, he didn't give up until it was done. And this case was far from done.

She curled her legs beneath her on the sofa and stroked Mr. Tiddles, who having spent two nights at Daisy's house decided he preferred it to his own home, even though Moira was back from her sister's.

"It's a common enough scam. He donates the dirty money to the charity, who put it through their books as a donation, but instead of keeping it all, they agree to pay him a portion of it back again."

"But why would they do that?" Daisy said. "It would be putting the charity at risk of legal action."

"Indeed, but it means they receive a donation that they otherwise would not have got. In some cases, such as this, it can run into hundreds of thousands of pounds per annum."

"Heavens," breathed Daisy. "Lightman was helping Thomas launder his ill-gotten gains in exchange for a hefty donation."

"That's it. From what we can gather, Rising Star received fifty percent of the funds. That was obviously their deal, until the donations dried up when Thomas disappeared."

Daisy paused, her brain ticking over. "It can't be Lightman who's the killer, then. He wouldn't want to jeopardize the money the charity was getting."

"That's a good point, but regardless of whether he's the murderer or not, he's still guilty of committing fraud."

"Have you traced the money back to Thomas's account?" Daisy wanted to know. They needed proof if they were going to arrest Lightman. No wonder he was drowning his sorrows over dinner. That might have been his last meal as a free man.

"Not to Thomas's account," McGuinness said. "To his wife, Hannah's."

"Oh my gosh." A shock wave went through her as she thought of the pregnant mother. "Do you think she's involved?"

"I don't know. I'm going to bring her in for questioning tomorrow." He hesitated. "Do you want to come in?"

"You'd let me sit in on the interview?" Daisy was surprised. She'd expected him to exclude her from the investigation from now on.

"I'd let you observe," he corrected. "There's a difference. You wouldn't be in the interview room."

"Ah, I'd be spying through the two-way mirror?"

He chuckled. "Something like that. If you're free, that is?"

"I'm free," she said quickly. "We're closed tomorrow. By the way, I don't think Hannah is going to be too pleased to be hauled in for questioning on Christmas Eve."

"A homicide investigation doesn't get put on hold just because it's the holidays," he said defensively. "But if you don't want to come, that's fine."

"I'll be there," she cut in. "Just give me a time."

"I'll let you know," he said.

Mr. Tiddles mewed contentedly. Daisy wished she felt as relaxed. Was it possible Hannah had another motive for killing her husband? Perhaps he had threatened to move the money out of her account and she wanted to hold on to it. That way, she'd get Clive and the laundered funds and Thomas would be out of their lives for good. It was a win-win-win.

"Did you have a good evening?" McGuinness asked, breaking into her musings.

It took her a moment to realize he was talking about the restaurant. "Oh, yes, it was lovely, thank you."

"Anyone I know?"

Daisy couldn't resist a smile at his fishing attempt. For a detective, he wasn't very subtle, but that wasn't his strong point. He preferred to blazon it out across an interrogation table.

"I was with Floria and Mimi. We had a girl's night out."

"That's good. I mean, that sounds like fun." Was that relief in his tone? Had he thought she might be on a date? A warmth spread through her body.

"I'll see you tomorrow, Paul." There was a smile on her face as she hung up.

Daisy arrived at Guildford police station at quarter to ten the following morning. McGuinness had texted her and told her to be there at ten for the interrogation. She gave the duty sergeant her name and he came out of his office and ushered her through to a sparse waiting room with no windows, uncomfortable plastic chairs, and cheap, linoleum tiling on the floor. Clearly, the police didn't want their witnesses or suspects getting too comfortable, or perhaps this was a reminder of what was to come if they didn't tell the truth. Taking a seat, she read the wanted posters and other police bulletins on the wall while she waited for McGuinness to come and get her.

At five to ten, a police sergeant she didn't recognize opened the door. "Miss Thorne, if you'll come with me, please?"

She got up and followed him down a long corridor and into a dark viewing room. She blinked as her eyes adjusted. She focused on the one-way window that looked into the sparse interrogation room, which far from being dark, was flooded with bright, fluorescent light. Daisy shivered involuntarily. She remembered what it felt like to be sitting right where Hannah Collington was now. The poor woman looked terrified and Daisy imagined she'd been hauled out of bed to the station without any warning. Her face was devoid of makeup, her hair unstyled, and one hand rested protectively on her swollen belly.

Facing her, his back to the window, was the stiff form of DCI McGuinness. His broad shoulders were tense and she could see the muscles strain in his neck as he leaned forward to speak to her. He was casually dressed in jeans and a shirt, despite the freezing temperature in the small room. Hannah was still wearing her long, winter coat.

He introduced his suspect for the purposes of the recording and reminded her she was being questioned under caution. Her eyes, round and terrified, were fixed on the detective's face.

"This is one of your bank accounts," he began, sliding a piece of paper across the steel table toward her. She glanced down at it. "Do you confirm that it is in your name?"

She frowned. "I don't bank at Barclays."

"As you can see, Mrs. Collington, the account is regis-tered in your name."

She picked it up and squinted at the writing at the top. "Yes, I can see that, but I didn't open this account."

"Are you saying your late husband opened this ac-count in your name?"

She shrugged. "He must have done. Like I said, I don't bank at Barclays. I've never seen this account before in my life."

"It's got ninety-two thousand pounds in it."

She gasped, as did Daisy. That was a lot of laundered money.

"Do you deny any knowledge of this account?"

"Of course. I didn't know it existed. If my husband was using it for business, he didn't tell me."

"It wasn't used for business, Mrs. Collington," McGuin-ness said. "It was used as a holding account for funds from Rising Star charity. Funds that Bas Lightman laun-dered for your husband."

"What?" She paled as she stared at him. "Laundered funds, did you say?"

He leaned forward in his chair. "Can you explain that?"

"I—no, I can't." She fell silent, her hand over her mouth.

"She's lying," Daisy muttered. The sergeant beside her shot her a strange look.

"Did you know about your husband's fraudulent activities?" By the stance of his body, Daisy knew McGuinness was fixing her with his steely, thousand-yard stare.

Hannah twisted in her chair. Yep, that stare had that effect on almost everyone.

"Mrs. Collington, if you withhold information from the police, you will be charged with obstructing the course of justice and possibly even aiding and abetting your husband. There will be jail time involved. I don't think you want to do that to your children. If you know anything, now would be a good time to speak up."

Still she hesitated, but her eyes filled with tears. Giving birth in jail was not an option any mother wanted to consider. Daisy knew it was only a matter of time before she caved.

"Okay, have it your way." McGuinness stood up and made to exit the room. "A booking sergeant will be here shortly to arrest you."

"Wait . . ." Her voice had a weak, plaintive ring to it.

McGuinness paused.

"I'll tell you what I know."

He nodded and sat down again. Daisy suppressed a grin. This was McGuinness's strength. Here, in the interrogation room, he was in his element.

She took a deep, quivering breath. "I knew my husband's business affairs weren't always aboveboard. That's why we left Glasgow in the first place. Some investment scheme he was running had collapsed and hundreds of people lost money."

"What kind of investment scheme?" McGuinness asked. For some reason—maybe it was the tone of his voice—Daisy got the impression he knew more about it than he let on. She remembered learning in her criminology diploma that detectives often asked questions they already knew the answer to. It helped them trick the suspect into confessing.

She hesitated. "It was property investment, although he didn't tell me the details. I only know that when it collapsed, we had to leave in a hurry. I didn't even have time to pack up the house." This was a bone of contention for Hannah, Daisy could tell. Even now, she was bitter about it. "I left so many of my possessions behind." She supposed that's what happened when you married a crook.

"Is that why he changed his name?" McGuinness asked. Daisy raised her eyebrows. It was starting to make sense now.

"Yes, he used to be Thomas Macpherson, but he changed it to Pierce when we got to Surrey. He said it would be a fresh start." The tears that had threatened to fall did so now and ran silently down her cheeks. Daisy almost felt sorry for her.

"But it wasn't a fresh start, was it?" McGuinness inquired. "He was still involved in fraudulent activities."

"Was he?" She shook her head. "He said he'd given all that up and I believed him. The real estate agency was a legitimate business venture. Clive would never be involved with anything illegal. He's a good man." Her eyes begged him to understand.

"Were you aware your husband was donating ten thousand pounds a month to the Rising Star charity? Where did that money come from?"

Her mouth fell open. "I honestly don't know. We didn't have that kind of money. We were paying off a mortgage on the house."

Daisy frowned. Could the money be from previous scams that he'd stashed away until he could launder it? It was possible, but it was an awful lot of cash to be holding on to. If the payments stopped when Thomas disappeared, then where was the rest of it?

Chapter 17

After the interview, McGuinness took Daisy up to his office. They walked through an open-plan squad room with a flat-screen television mounted to the wall. It was set on a news channel with the sound muted. She felt the eyes of the other detectives on her as she followed him into a corner office with glass windows overlooking Guildford Town center. McGuinness closed the blinds to give them some privacy.

"I've released Hannah Collington," he told her, easing his tall frame into the leather swivel chair behind the desk. There was a standard-issue computer between them, which he pushed to one side so he could see her better. On his desk were a pile of case files, many dog-eared, as well as two empty coffee cups. His desk was pretty much as she'd imagined.

"Do you believe she had no knowledge of her husband's activities?" Daisy asked.

He shrugged. "I think she knew what was going on in Scotland, but perhaps not since they moved to Surrey, or maybe she wanted to believe he'd given all that up. The Scottish authorities passed on his file to me. Thomas Macpherson ran a property investment portfolio that collapsed, depriving hundreds of people, mostly pensioners, of their life savings."

"That's terrible. Was he arrested for it?"

"No, they couldn't prove it was a scam, although the reported losses were in the millions. Macpherson walked free, but was told he could no longer operate the scheme in the country."

"So he moved to England," Daisy finished. "Do you think he was still running it here?"

"Not that we can make out," McGuinness told her, leaning back in his chair. "However, that money he was donating must have come from somewhere."

"I was thinking about that," Daisy said, causing McGuinness to smile. "What if he kept those millions hidden away and was slowly laundering it via the charity?"

"I'd say that's a safe bet," McGuinness agreed. "The question is, Where? He didn't use a legitimate bank account, because we would have spotted it. His wife's account has been suspended and that money will have to go back to the defrauded investors, although I suspect it's a little too late for many of them."

Daisy could only imagine what it must feel like to lose everything. Then a thought struck her. "Do you think one of the people he scammed could have killed him?"

McGuinness hunched forward. "It's definitely one line of inquiry."

"I can help," she offered.

He gave her a sideways glance. "Daisy . . ."

She held up a hand. "I meant an internet search, that's all. I promise I won't talk to anyone." She gave him a coquettish smile. "That's your job, Detective."

He raised an eyebrow. "Are you patronizing me?"

"I wouldn't dream of it."

He couldn't help smiling. "Okay, but let me know if you discover anything of value. I have a team going through the list of defrauded investors."

"List?" Her eyebrows shot up. "Is there any chance of having a peek?"

"Sorry, Daisy. I can't let you see it. There are privacy issues around sharing that kind of information with civilians, even those consulting for the police."

"I understand." That was unfortunate. A list would have made her search a lot easier.

McGuinness's desk phone and his mobile rang at the same time, and a few seconds later there was a knock on his door. "Guv, we need you in the briefing room."

"Right." He shot Daisy an apologetic look. "I've got to get going."

"That's okay." She got to her feet. "I can see myself out."

"Call you later."

Before she could answer, he was striding out of the office, his phone to his ear, the one on the desk ringing unanswered.

* * *

Daisy was on the motorway back to Edgemead when a thought occurred to her. Maybe Thomas Pierce had stashed the money at Holly Lodge. It was the perfect location—an empty, run-down house. It was too expensive to sell, and needed a heck of a lot of work done to it, which didn't make it a very likely sale prospect. Perhaps he'd taken advantage of that to hide the money there. He'd have a key, since it was on his books. Was that what he had been doing there on Christmas Eve?

She rang Floria, using the car's Bluetooth function so she didn't have to hold the phone to her ear. "I need to go to Holly Lodge and take another look around," she told her. "Could you meet me there with the key?"

"I'm at work." Floria sounded disappointed. "I'm prepping for my event on Boxing Day, but Mimi is at Brompton Court. I'm sure she won't mind meeting you there."

"Okay, great."

Daisy rang Mimi, who was only too happy to let Daisy into Holly Lodge. "I want to measure up for the new kitchen units," she said. "But I've been too nervous to go there by myself until the murderer is caught."

They met an hour later at the pretty, tumbledown property. The fields around it were still blanketed in snow, and white powder lay undisturbed on the roof of the lodge as well as the thick holly bushes that surrounded it. It was so picturesque that it was hard to believe a body had been found here the week before.

"I can't wait to get these renovations finished," Mimi admitted to Daisy as they stood outside looking up at the property. "Brompton Court is wonderful, but it's so big and drafty and I can't help feeling Mother's ghost is lurking around, criticizing my every move."

Daisy laughed. "I wouldn't be surprised. She had a knack for doing that."

"Was she really terrible?" Mimi asked, taking Daisy by surprise. "I only ask because Floria is reluctant to speak badly of her to spare my feelings, but I know she had an awful time of it growing up. You knew Serena. Was she really the tyrant people make her out to be?"

Daisy bit her lip. If Floria had masked Serena's true nature to protect her half-sister, then it wasn't Daisy's place to spoil that, but Mimi sensed her hesitation.

"Tell me the truth, Daisy. I never met her, so it makes no difference to me."

Daisy took a deep breath. "Well, she wouldn't have won any parenting prizes. Floria spent most of her childhood at boarding school or with nannies. Violeta, the housekeeper, practically raised her. Serena was never home, thanks to her busy touring schedule, and when her career stalled later in life, she reacted by throwing elaborate parties and dating unsuitable men."

"That's where Floria got her party-planning skills," Mimi remarked, but her eyes were sad.

"Yes, Serena left most of the planning to Floria, even though she barely acknowledged her presence. I don't think Serena even knew my name and I was often at Brompton Court with Floria in the latter years."

Mimi shook her head. "Unbelievable. I used to blame my parents for not telling me who my birth mother was, but now I see how lucky I was to have them. They may not have known how to handle me, but at least they cared."

"Floria had no one," Daisy told her. "Her father was constantly on tour with Serena as her manager and when they split up, he retired to his villa in the south of France. He seemed to forget he had a daughter who needed him."

"Poor Floria." Mimi wrung her hands. "At least she's got Josh now."

"Yes, and they're perfect for each other."

"I was there the night they met," Mimi confided. "He was still with his ex-girlfriend, Paloma, back then."

"The model?" Daisy had heard bits and pieces of the story.

"Yes, they'd been together for ages, but she was high maintenance; always had to be the center of attention. When I introduced him to Floria, they hit it off instantly, and I knew it was only a matter of time before they got together."

"Love at first sight," Daisy sighed.

"That's how it was for me and Rob too," Mimi's gaze softened. "As soon as I met him on the flight back to Australia after Serena's funeral, I knew . . . Even though it took several months for him to ask me out on a proper date."

How nice to have love fall into your lap like that. Daisy thought about McGuinness. The first time she'd met him, he'd told her point-blank not to get involved in a police investigation. No, it was safe to say that for them, it certainly hadn't been love at first sight. Not even like.

"But you and that handsome detective have something going on?" Mimi said, noticing Daisy's flushed face.

"Oh, no. We just work together."

Mimi tilted her head sideways. "I think it's a little more than that. I've seen the way he looks at you."

"Do you think so?" Daisy wasn't sure. There were moments when she felt there might be something there, like at the Christmas market, but for the most part, he treated her as a colleague, someone to discuss the case with.

"Definitely." Her green eyes sparkled. "You might have to make the first move, though. I don't think he's the type."

"Not unless you're a suspect in a murder investigation," Daisy said with a raised brow.

Mimi laughed. "Exactly, but I think you should go for it. He's keen, I can tell. You won't be disappointed."

Daisy bit her lip. Would she ever be brave enough to make the first move where McGuinness was concerned? After what had happened with Tim, she wasn't sure she'd ever be willing to put her heart on the line like that again. "I'll think about it."

Mimi opened the front door with a loud creak. "You do that. Now, what are we doing here?"

Daisy glanced around the entrance hall. The dust had settled since the chimney had caved in, but the floor was pockmarked by missing tiles that the workmen had already removed, making it look like a broken chessboard. The space created by the vast ceilings seemed sad, rather than grand, amplified by the peeling wallpaper and empty, derelict feel.

"I may have bitten off more than I can chew," Mimi said, walking into the living room. Daisy followed, trying to shrug off the grim memory of the body. It was brighter in here. Sunlight streamed in through the cracked windows and refracted onto the walls.

"It'll be lovely once it's finished," Daisy told her.

"I know." She stared up at the dusty chandelier. "We've been told we can't resume the renovations until after the case is solved and goodness knows when that'll be."

Daisy had suspected as much. She turned to Mimi. "Maybe you can help me solve it, then."

Mimi perked up. "Tell me how."

"The man who was killed here, Thomas Pierce, was a con man. He swindled hundreds of people out of their life savings in a dummy investment scheme."

"That's awful," Mimi gasped.

"He laundered almost a hundred thousand pounds of it, but we think there was way more than that to start with."

"You think it's hidden here?" Mimi's face lit up. "At Holly Lodge?"

"It's one theory," Daisy said. "The house was abandoned and would have made an ideal hiding place. No one came here unless they were being shown around by Thomas or Clive, the real estate agents."

"And they were the only ones with a key," Mimi finished, glancing around her. "I wonder where he could have hidden it?"

"I thought maybe we could have a look around," Daisy suggested. "I know the police have searched the place, but they were looking for a second body, not a briefcase or box of money."

"You think it's cash?" Mimi asked.

Daisy pursed her lips. "I'm not sure. It needed to be liquid enough that he could donate ten thousand a month to the Rising Star charity, so I don't see how it can be anything else. If he'd bought diamonds or art or anything like that, he'd have to fence it before he could sell it and that would take time. He seemed to have a ready amount of cash to donate."

"I agree," Mimi said. "Cash seems the most obvious. Let's get searching."

Daisy took downstairs while Mimi searched the upstairs bedrooms and bathroom. An hour later, they were still at it. Eventually, Mimi came downstairs covered in dust. "No luck. If it is here, I don't think it's upstairs. I've searched in every nook and cranny. I even pried up some loose floorboards."

Daisy swept her hair off her face and grimaced as particles of dust, soot, and even a cobweb fell out. "I was so sure it was here somewhere," she croaked.

"Let's have a cup of tea and regroup," Mimi suggested, brushing the dirt off her jeans. "I think there's a box left over from when we were here last."

They traipsed into the kitchen and Daisy sat down at the wonky table, while Mimi filled the kettle and turned it on. At least the electricity was working.

"It's freezing." Mimi rubbed her hands together. "I'm not used to this weather. Did you know that it's the middle of summer in Australia, right now? I wonder if we can put the heating on? My hands are like ice blocks."

"You'll have to restart the boiler." Daisy knew Mimi wouldn't be familiar with the way things worked in the UK, having come from Australia where radiators were rarely necessary. The wooden chair creaked as she got up. "I'll see if I can do it."

She opened a cupboard that looked like it might house the boiler. "Yep, here it is. It's a beast of a thing and doesn't look like it's been used in decades, so don't hold your breath."

She switched on the electricity supply and then turned the knob to the *on* position. Nothing happened.

"It's completely dead," Daisy said. "You'll have to get the electrician to look at it when he's next here."

Mimi sank into a chair. "Another thing to add to my to-do list."

The kettle clicked off and Daisy made them each a cup of tea. Mimi immediately wrapped her hands around it. "That's better. I don't know how you cope in this climate."

Daisy sat down opposite her. "You get used to it and once the boiler's working, the house will be toasty warm."

They discussed the missing money. "I've looked everywhere I can think of," Daisy said wearily. "Up the chimney, in the pantry, under the broken floorboards, behind the paneling. Nothing. Maybe I got it wrong? Perhaps it's not here at all."

"Do you think he buried it outside?" Mimi turned her head to look out the dirty kitchen window.

"It's possible. Unfortunately, we don't have time to go digging up the garden."

"The wife could be holding on to it," Mimi suggested.

Daisy gnawed on her lower lip. "I suppose so." She threw her hands in the air. "Oh, I don't know what to think anymore." She was out of ideas.

They finished their tea, washed up, and left the house. As they drove away, Daisy glanced back in her rearview mirror at the silent, glistening lodge. Somehow, she'd have to find a way to get it to reveal its secrets.

Chapter 18

Daisy knew what she was doing was wrong. DCI McGuinness would be furious if he found out, which was why he mustn't, not unless her hunch paid off. After she'd disregarded his instructions the day Wendy had been murdered, she'd vowed not to take matters into her own hands again. But this was the exception.

Waterloo was one of the busiest railway stations in London and today was no exception. It was heaving with commuters eager to get home after a long day in the city. The public address system broadcast delays to trains and last-minute changes, and passengers surged toward the platforms with every new announcement. It was dark when Daisy left the station, the winter sun having set almost an hour ago. She looked around, got her bearings, then set off up The Cut. The commercial street ran from

Waterloo station to Southwark, where Borough Market was located. Dotted along each side were trendy bars and restaurants, all of which were decorated with elaborate bunting, lighting, and festive props.

"Come on in, love," called a man standing next to a blow-up Santa, drinking a pint of lager and smoking a cigarette. "You look like you could do with a drink."

She shot him a polite smile, but shook her head and continued up the road.

Lilly Rosewood, now Westerford, worked at Borough Market, a vibey, artisan food market situated near London Bridge.

Daisy had managed to find the ex-barmaid's business address online using the details McGuinness had given her. It turned out Lilly was part owner in her husband's bakery, an artisan enterprise called Knead Me, based in the market itself. They sold everything from sourdough to croissants and by the comments on their Instagram account, were very popular with the locals.

It was after five o'clock, but the market closed later in the run up to Christmas, so she was confident they'd still be open. After searching the mouthwatering array of stalls, she finally found one with a rustic *Knead Me* sign hanging above it. The counter had a few loaves of sourdough, rye, and spelt bread left on it, along with some *pain au chocolat* and two croissants.

"It smells so good," Daisy complimented a petite brunette in an apron standing behind the counter. The man next to her was busy serving a customer.

"Thanks." She broke into an infectious smile. "Can I help you?"

"I'll take a loaf of your sourdough." Daisy's mouth was watering just looking at it.

"Good choice." The woman reached for it with a gloved hand. "It's our most popular item. We're known for it around here."

"I'm sure." Daisy paid and the woman handed her the bread in a brown paper bag. "Thank you. I'm sorry, I hope you don't think I'm rude, but are you Lilly?"

The woman's blue eyes twinkled. "Yes, have we met?"

"No, we haven't, but I work with Detective McGuinness from Guildford CID. I wonder if I could have a private word?" She cringed inwardly. McGuinness wouldn't appreciate her bandying his name around.

The friendly smile vanished as the blue eyes narrowed. "I've already told that inspector everything I know about Thomas."

Daisy kept her voice light. "I know, but I have a theory I'd like to run by you."

"Are you a detective too?" The woman glanced at her jeans, sneakers, and winter coat.

"No, I'm a—consultant. Would you mind? It won't take long."

Her husband glanced over. "All right, love?"

Lilly wiped her hands on her apron. "Sure, give me a moment."

Daisy gestured to a vacant wooden table, one of the many dotted around the market square. "I'll wait over here."

Lilly said something to her husband, gestured to Daisy, and then came over. "I don't have long. We have to cash up soon."

Daisy got straight to it. "I know you told DCI McGuinness that your affair with Thomas Pierce was over."

Her expression was guarded. "Yeah, he broke up with me to go back to his wife."

Daisy studied her. "Except he didn't, did he?"

Lilly looked startled, then abashed, and Daisy knew her hunch had been right. "He was going to leave his wife for you, wasn't he?"

"Yes, but you can't tell anyone." She cast a furtive glance at her husband.

"Why did you lie to the police?" Daisy asked.

Lilly folded her hands in her lap. "I didn't want people to think I was the evil party. When I found out Tom had been murdered, I thought it best if I said he'd dumped me. It would give me a good reason for leaving."

"It also gave you a motive," Daisy pointed out.

She hung her head. "I didn't think of that."

There was a brief pause. "Why did you leave, then?" Daisy wanted to know.

Lilly's voice dropped to a whisper. "We were going to run away together on Christmas Day. It was all organized. He'd meet me at the station at ten in the morning and we'd get the train to Waterloo, then catch the Eurostar to Europe. No one would ever find us. He said he had enough money for us to start over." Her face clouded over. "I believed him."

"What happened?" Daisy asked, but she already knew the answer.

"I waited at the station but he didn't come. I'd packed up, walked out on my job, given up my flat—I had nothing to stay for. I waited for hours and tried repeatedly to get hold of him, but there was no answer. I thought he'd given up on us or changed his mind." She swallowed. "I had nowhere to go, so I got on the train anyway and stayed at an Airbnb for a couple of days while I tried to contact him."

"Except you couldn't."

Lilly shook her head. "No, I even called his home, which he'd told me never to do, and his wife picked up. I asked to speak to him but she just hung up on me. I figured he'd decided to stay with her. I never in a million years imagined he was dead."

Daisy digested all this. So Thomas had been willing to leave his wife and young child to run off with his mistress. "Did he say how much money he had or where he'd got it from?" Daisy asked.

Lilly's brow creased. "I think he said it was his savings, but I can't remember. It was a long time ago and I've moved on since then. I put Thomas out of my mind and found a job at a local bakery. That's how I met Justin. Then last year we decided to launch Knead Me." She waved at the stall and her face lit up. It was clear she loved what she did.

"I'm glad things worked out for you," Daisy said.

Lilly gazed lovingly at her husband. "Thank you. Yes, they did. It's weird to think if that hadn't happened with Tom, I would never have found my soul mate."

"Life has a funny way of working out," Daisy said softly.

Lilly glanced up. "Is that all? I have to get back."

"That's all. Thanks for speaking with me."

Daisy spent another hour browsing the market stalls and before she left, she'd bought several different cheeses, a jar of olives, some sun-dried tomatoes, and a small packet of authentic Turkish delight. Dinner tonight was going to be a feast. On a whim, she dialed McGuinness's number on the train home. "Are you free tonight?" she asked him.

"I'm still at work," was his terse reply.

Daisy hesitated, then remembered Mimi's words.

"I've got some lovely fresh bread and an assortment of cheeses for supper," she said. "I was wondering if you wanted to join me?" She could fill him in on her evening adventure at the same time, or maybe she'd wait until after he'd eaten. He would be less inclined to get indigestion, that way. Once again, she'd gone behind his back and taken matters into her own hands. If he was going to be angry, the least she could do was to feed him first.

He hesitated.

Daisy held her breath.

"Um . . . okay, sure. Give me an hour and I'll be there."

She breathed out. "See you then."

Chapter 19

McGuinness arrived at Daisy's cottage shortly before nine o'clock. It was later than Daisy usually ate, but she didn't mind waiting. She knew he'd got away as soon as he could. He had a tendency to bury himself in his work and not come up for air. If she hadn't called, he'd probably have kept going until he couldn't keep his eyes open any longer. The break would do him good.

"Long day?" she asked, after she opened the door.

He rolled his eyes. "It never ends. It must be something about this time of year. It's like all the crazies come out and decide to cause havoc."

She stood back to let him in. "You've got more than one case on the go?"

He took off his jacket. "Currently, I'm dealing with two

burglaries and an armed robbery on top of this double-homicide. Plus, we're short-staffed due to the holidays."

Daisy sympathized. He did look a little ragged around the edges. "Well, you can relax now. I've got a mini-feast lined up for us."

He caught sight of the Christmas tree sparkling merrily in front of the window. "You've been busy."

She tilted her head and admired the tree. "Yes, Frank the florist dropped it off for me this afternoon. I bumped into him a few days ago and told him I hadn't got one yet."

"It's beautiful." He walked closer to admire the tinsel, glittering baubles, and twinkling lights. Daisy had hauled her Christmas decorations down from the attic and spent a lovely few hours before he'd arrived decorating it. There were still a few left in the box.

"Why don't you put up one?" she suggested. "It's Christmas, after all."

Without speaking, he selected a little cupid and hung it on a branch. "I never did manage to get a tree this year," he admitted. "I've been too busy to think about Christmas."

"You can share mine." She handed him a glass of wine. "I thought I was too late, but then Frank dropped this one off. I'm so grateful, I've never not had a tree before. It seems wrong, somehow. Come and sit down, you must be starving."

He patted his stomach. "I am hungry. It's been a long day." He surveyed the spread. "This looks great."

She avoided his gaze. "I popped to the market this evening."

He read the label on the side of the olive jar and his

eyes narrowed. "You went to Borough Market? That's quite a trek, isn't it?"

She ought to have known he'd figure it out. She felt her cheeks grow hot. "Why don't you sit down and have a glass of wine and I'll tell you all about it."

He gave her a wary look. "Daisy?"

She picked up a knife and began cutting the bread.

"Tell me," he said, his wine untouched.

She grimaced. "Okay, but promise you won't be mad?"

"Now you're making me very worried."

She put a thick slice of the sourdough on a plate and handed it to him. He took it without comment, his gray eyes focused on her face.

She put the knife down. "Okay, I went to visit Lilly Westerford."

He set his plate down. "I knew it! How many times do I have to tell you not to talk to suspects?"

She held up a hand. "I know, but hear me out. This is important."

He gestured for her to continue, but she read the disappointment in his face.

"Thomas didn't dump Lilly," Daisy said. "They *were* going to run away together. Thomas told her he had money saved. Their plan was to go to Europe and start a new life together."

"Money saved?" He frowned.

"Yes, although it's more likely to be the ill-gotten gains from that investment scam, which he'd hidden away somewhere."

McGuinness fell silent. Daisy let him ponder this while she laid out the cheeses and other delicacies. When he spoke, his voice was low. "You think he hid the money at Holly Lodge, don't you?"

Daisy grinned. He'd connected the dots fast.

He studied her. "And I bet you've already searched it." At her guilty look he added, "Don't tell me you've found the missing funds?"

"Sadly, no, but you're half right. I did search the lodge with Mimi this morning, but we didn't find anything."

"That doesn't mean it's not there. You might be on to something."

"I know, but we looked everywhere and couldn't find it."

McGuinness took a sip of his wine and then cut a large chunk of brie, which he spread on his bread. "I can't believe Lilly lied to me. Why would she say they'd broken up, if they hadn't?"

"She didn't want people to think badly of her," Daisy explained. "She waited for Thomas on the platform, but when he didn't arrive, she assumed he'd changed his mind and had decided to stay with his wife. So she left by herself."

"How did you know she was lying?" McGuinness mumbled, his mouth full.

"It was a hunch," Daisy told him. "Thomas and Hannah's marriage was in tatters, and I got the impression Hannah wouldn't have wanted him back, even if he'd asked. She was in love with Clive by then. And everybody kept saying how nice Lilly was, so I figured, Why would he dump her and go back to an unhappy marriage?"

McGuinness watched her contemplatively. "Because of the baby."

She shrugged. "Maybe. I still thought it was worth checking out." When he didn't reply, she continued. "And when we discovered the missing funds might be out there somewhere, I wondered whether Lilly had taken it."

"And?" He raised an eyebrow.

"She had no knowledge of it. She thought the money was coming from his savings. What everyone says is true. Lilly is a nice person and I don't think she had anything to do with Thomas's murder."

"Still, I'm going to have to get her to come in and re-vise her statement," he said with a frown. Daisy could tell he was annoyed he hadn't picked up that Lilly had been lying to him. Interrogations were supposed to be his strong suit, but sometimes, Daisy mused, you caught more flies with honey. A principle McGuinness hadn't quite mastered yet.

After they'd eaten, Daisy made a pot of coffee and they sat in the lounge, the radio playing softly in the background. McGuinness seemed more relaxed now. His shoulders were less tense and his face had lost that pinched expression. Daisy admired the way he filled the armchair, his long legs stretched out in front of him.

"Thanks for the supper. It was just what I needed to recharge my batteries."

She handed him a cup of coffee. "I'm glad. I thought you could do with some sustenance."

He gazed at her and she felt her heart skip a beat. "No Mr. Tiddles tonight?"

She chuckled. "No, Moira convinced him to go home with some expensive cat treats."

She was about to turn around and sit down on the sofa when he reached out and took her arm. "Daisy, I want you to be careful, okay? I know we've got this working relationship now, but I would hate it if anything happened to you."

"You would?" She tried to read the expression on his face.

He drew her down toward him until she was perched
on his lap. "It happened once before. I lost someone I
cared about and I don't think I could go through that
again."

"You lost someone during an investigation?" she
asked, gazing up at him. He'd never mentioned anything
about this to her before.

A muscle in his jaw tensed. "Yeah, it was a long time
ago and I don't want to talk about it, but please be careful. You've had a few close shaves in the past." His expression softened. "And you're very important to me."

"I am?"

"Yes, you are." He leaned forward. She held her
breath. His lips came down on hers.

Daisy gave herself up to his kiss and as it deepened,
she couldn't think of anywhere else she'd rather be. Her
heart hammered in her chest, but at the same time, it felt
so right. Her arm snaked around his neck and her hand
buried into his hair. He held her tightly against him. Kissing Paul was as wonderful as she'd always dreamed it
would be.

Eventually, he broke away, breathing a little heavily. "I
think I'd better go now." His eyes burned with an inten-
sity she'd never seen before.

Reluctantly, and a little weakly, she got off him so he
could get to his feet. "I'm really glad you came round
tonight, Paul."

He moved a stray hair out of her face. "I am too,
Daisy."

Chapter 20

Daisy decided not to tell anyone about that kiss, not even Floria. She wanted to keep it to herself for a while longer and bask in the memory of it. Besides, even though he'd kissed her, it didn't necessarily mean anything would come of it. McGuinness was a busy man and his attention was taken up by this case and the others he was running. She didn't kid herself that he had any extra time in his schedule for her. Once this investigation was over and the killer was safely behind bars, then they could see where they stood. Until then, it was safer if she kept what had happened to herself.

Today was Christmas Eve. Ooh La La was closed and wouldn't open again until the twenty-seventh. Three glorious days off. Daisy spent a luxurious morning pampering herself and was getting dressed when her phone buzzed. It was Floria.

"Daisy, you are coming to Christmas lunch tomorrow, aren't you? I'm finalizing the menu and I want to know how many mouths I have to feed."

Floria always went all-out, whether it was an intimate get-together or a full-scale launch party. "I wouldn't miss it for the world."

"Oh, wonderful." There was a pause and then Floria said, "Can I put DCI McGuinness down as your plus-one?"

Daisy froze. Had her friend found out about their kiss? "Why would you do that?" she blurted out.

Floria laughed. "Don't be silly, Dais. We all know you fancy him. Why don't you ask him to join us? I'm sure he'd appreciate it. I doubt they serve a Christmas roast at the precinct."

She had a point. Daisy felt bad for not inviting him earlier. Perhaps she should have said something last night. But no, the evening had been perfect the way it was.

"Oh, okay, but he might have other plans." It struck her that she didn't know whether he had family in the vicinity or friends that he'd made arrangements with already. He hadn't said a word about it to her.

"Well, never mind. I'll cater for him anyway and if he doesn't come, there'll just be more for us."

Daisy hung up and thought about asking Paul to Christmas dinner. Was it too soon? He might think she was rushing things by inviting him to such an important event. She was debating what to do when she saw his name flash up on her screen and her pulse raced.

"Hi, Paul." She tried to keep her tone upbeat and friendly.

"Hello, Daisy." His was softer, warmer than usual. A delicious shiver shot through her. "I'm just calling to let you know I've arrested Bas Lightman."

"What? Did he confess?" All thoughts of last night flew from her mind. Was Lightman the murderer?

"No, I've arrested him for fraud. He admitted to assisting Thomas Pierce in laundering the funds. He said Thomas approached him with the deal after wining and dining him for several weeks. The charity needed the money, so Lightman agreed."

"I can sort of understand where he's coming from," Daisy said. "He did it for a good cause."

McGuinness grunted. "He broke the law and now he's got to pay for it. He'll probably get some jail time, but it won't be much, and he'll have to pay a fine as well as give the stolen money back."

"What will happen to the charity?" Daisy asked.

"They'll get some bad press, but they'll survive. I'm sure someone else will take up the reins, probably his undersecretary, a man called Mark Avery." Daisy thought back to the restaurant. Mark Avery must have been the man with the goatee. He seemed a reliable sort. He'd certainly been able to handle his inebriated boss with a minimum of fuss. Maybe it would turn out all right.

"Okay, well, that's good," Daisy said.

"I just thought I'd let you know."

She hesitated. It was on the tip of her tongue to invite him to Floria's Christmas lunch, but something held her back. "Thanks, Paul," she said eventually. "I appreciate you keeping me in the loop."

"I'll call you later." And he was gone.

Daisy stared out of the window. It was snowing again, but not a blizzard like before. This time it was a soft flurry of snowflakes that fell on the already white landscape. The sky had turned silver like the color of Paul's eyes. It was mesmerizing. She blinked and drew herself back to the present. There was Christmas shopping to be done and as usual, she'd left it until the last minute.

Should she get Paul a gift? She bit her lip. Would he get her one? If she'd invited him to the Christmas lunch tomorrow he may have, but now he'd be caught unprepared. He was even busier than she was, so she doubted he'd have the time to go shopping.

She grimaced. Why was she such a coward?

A kiss was one thing, but spending Christmas together was something else entirely. That said "we're a couple" and she wasn't sure that they were. Not in the traditional sense.

She turned away from the window. Maybe she'd get him something small anyway, just in case. After all, she might change her mind and invite him. There was still time.

The High Street was bustling with shoppers. Christmas lights beckoned in shop windows and everywhere Christmas music was playing. Miraculously, she'd managed to get everybody on her list a present, except for Paul. What did you buy a grumpy, overworked detective for Christmas? The usual cheesy gifts sprung to mind. No, she wanted to get him something special. Small, but significant.

"Last-minute panic buying?" came a deep voice from behind her. She spun around and saw Josh, Floria's husband, standing there looking sheepish.

"You too?" She eyed the packages in his hands.

He raised his arms. "I got Floria something weeks ago, but now I find out we've got a full house for Christmas, so I thought I'd better stock up on a few more items."

"Don't get anything for me," she told him. "It's not necessary."

"Too late," he retorted, breaking into a lopsided grin. "Already done. Tell me, is your brooding detective coming?"

She laughed. "You've been talking to Floria."

He raised his eyebrows.

"I haven't invited him yet, if that's what you mean."

"Why not?"

She shuffled her feet in the snow. "I don't know. Maybe I'm scared he'll say yes."

Josh studied her. "Don't you want to spend Christmas Day with him?"

"I do. That's the problem."

"Ah." His face relaxed in understanding. "Well, if it's any consolation, I think he's a great guy and you two make a cute couple."

Daisy flushed. "Thanks, but I still don't—"

"Best to strike while the iron's hot." He nudged her with his elbow. "I did with Floria and I don't regret it for a second, even though it was terrifying at the time."

Daisy gulped. It *was* terrifying. She'd been burned once before and she didn't fancy going through that again, but perhaps she was reading too much into this. They'd only shared a kiss, nothing more than that, and he might already have plans.

Josh gestured to the bags in his hands. "I've got to get a move on. Looking forward to seeing you both tomorrow."

Daisy shook her head as she watched him walk away.

She was inside the coffee shop warming up when her eye caught sight of the novelty store across the road and she had a brain wave. She knew exactly what she was going to get Paul. Smiling to herself, she finished her latte and crossed the street to the parade of shops on the other side.

It was when she was coming out that she ran into Krish. He had his arms full of bags and nearly bumped into her. "Oh, sorry Dais, I didn't see you there."

"I'm not surprised." She surveyed his mound of parcels. "You've been busy."

"I'm staying with Douglas," he said. "My boiler packed up and I can't get a repairman in until after Christmas."

"You don't seem too upset," Daisy said.

Krish beamed. "No, I'm not. The only problem is his entire family is coming over and he's got three sisters and two brothers. Who has six children?" He shook his head in amazement.

Daisy laughed. "Good luck with that."

They chatted for a while longer, then the bus arrived and Krish hopped on, leaving Daisy to make her way back home. It was still snowing, but it wasn't wet or driving snow, just a fluttering like in a snow globe. As she walked down the lane to her house, she felt a surge of Christmas spirit for the first time since Thomas Pierce's body had been discovered.

Still in a good mood, she let herself in and turned the radio on, then set about unpacking her shopping. Tonight, she'd wrap all the presents to take to Brompton Court tomorrow. She loved that ritual. There was something so therapeutic about wrapping gifts bought for friends and family, tying little bows in the ribbons and writing out the cards in neat, cursive handwriting with Christmas music playing softly in the background.

Her Christmas tree sparkled cheerily and she thought about how Paul had picked the cupid out of the box. Had he had love on his mind? Then she chastised herself for being overly sentimental. It was sheer coincidence he'd picked that bauble out of the box. He'd been so busy, he hadn't even got a tree. Christmas—and love—was probably the last thing on his mind.

Turning her thoughts to the investigation, she wondered how he was getting on with the list of people that Thomas Pierce had swindled. She itched to call him and find out, but something told her not to. He'd let her know if there were any developments, and if she didn't speak to him, she wasn't in danger of inviting him to Christmas lunch.

Ignoring the voice in her head that yelled *coward*, she made herself a hot chocolate and sat at her kitchen counter with her laptop, singing along to "Last Christmas" by Wham! Turning it on, she did an internet search for Thomas Macpherson and waited see what came up. Her eyes ran down the list of results. There was a soccer coach by that name, as well as a television presenter, but the third search result was an article in a Scottish paper about the property investment scam.

There were several comments by angry individuals who had lost their savings, but nothing with any real menace. The photograph supplied was of an elderly woman standing outside a house with a *For Sale* sign in front of it. "*Widow, Mrs. Persephone Williams*," Daisy read out loud, "*lost everything and was forced to sell her family home in Glasgow*."

Poor woman. She grimaced in sympathy and then something caught her eye. She stared at the woman's hand. The photograph was black-and-white so it was hard to be certain, but Daisy was sure she'd seen that ring before. She zoomed in on the photograph, but the picture pixelated, so she zoomed out again. Jumping up, she opened a drawer in the bureau and took out a magnifying glass. Dashing back to the laptop, she squinted through it at the picture on the screen. It was slightly clearer now, and yes, it looked incredibly similar to . . .

She sat back and gnawed on her lower lip. Was it possible? The timing fit, but she could be wrong. She had to be sure first, before she spoke to Paul.

Grabbing her phone, she dialed Floria's number. Her friend picked up on the second ring. "Daisy, hi. You caught me at a bad time. I'm just about to meet Anne-Marie, the National Trust lady at Holly Lodge."

Daisy froze as an icy chill slipped down her spine. "Floria, are you with Josh?"

"Josh? No, it's just me and Mimi. We're showing her the house."

"Is she there yet?"

"No, we're still waiting, but she should be here soon. Daisy, what's the matter?"

"Nothing, I'm on my way. I'll explain when I get there."

Chapter 21

Daisy grabbed her keys and phone and ran outside to her car. There was a mound of snow on the hood and the windshield was frosted over and impossible to see out of.

"Oh, no!" She sprinted back inside and filled a jug with lukewarm water from the tap. Dashing out again, she threw it over the front and back windows. There was no time to deice.

The Honda made deep grooves in the snow as she reversed out of the driveway. It slid as it tried to find traction, but eventually the tires gripped and she was off. She sped up the lane, carving deep striations in the powdery snow. Using her car's Bluetooth function, she dialed Paul's number but it diverted to voicemail.

Cursing under her breath, she left a message. "Paul, it's me. I'm on my way to Holly Lodge. I think I know who the killer is. Can you send a team over there right away? Mimi and Floria are in danger."

Next, she called Josh. Luckily, he picked up on the first ring.

"Daisy, everything okay?"

It hadn't been that long since she'd seen him in the High Street.

"Josh, I don't want to be overly dramatic, but could you come to Holly Lodge? I think Floria and Mimi might be in trouble."

"From who? The National Trust lady?" She could hear the confusion in his voice.

"Yes, no. I don't know. It's just a hunch. Could you come anyway, just to be on the safe side?"

"Sure, I'll leave right now. See you in twenty minutes."

"Thanks, Josh."

She turned onto the arterial road, which was clear of snow. Being well-used, the gutters had turned into rivers of dirty slush. Daisy drove as fast as she dared until she reached the Cobham Road. Here she had to reduce her speed again, but she stayed in the grooves made by Floria's MINI Cooper to prevent her little car from skidding off the road. There were deep, murky ditches on either side and she didn't want to end up in one of those.

Finally, with a sigh of relief, she turned into the winding driveway that led to Holly Lodge. Outside was Floria's car, as well as a rented Honda Civic.

Anne-Marie.

Daisy hoped she was wrong, but the ring on the hand of the old lady in the article was almost identical to the one Anne-Marie had been wearing at dinner the other night. She was sure of it.

Daisy burst in through the front door, only to find Floria, Mimi, and Anne-Marie talking in the living room. They were admiring the chandelier and all turned in astonishment as she rushed in.

"Daisy, are you all right?" Floria asked. "You sounded very cryptic on the phone."

Daisy's gaze fell on Anne-Marie's hand. There it was, the same fake emerald surrounded by a ring of diamanté that she'd seen in the article.

She paused to catch her breath. There was no imminent threat. Anne-Marie had no idea Daisy knew who she was, but all that was about to change. "Why didn't you tell us your mother-in-law was one of the victims of the property investment scheme run by Thomas Macpherson?" she asked the National Trust lady.

Anne-Marie stared at her. "I'm sorry, I don't understand."

"Your mother-in-law, Mrs. Persephone Williams. That is your husband's mother, isn't it?"

Anne-Marie nodded. "Yes, but she's dead. She passed away over three years ago."

"How did she die?" Daisy asked.

Floria frowned. "Daisy, what is this all about?"

Daisy held up a hand. "I'll explain in a minute, Flo. I'm sorry to burst in like this, but it's important."

Floria knew better than to argue with her friend, so she turned to Anne-Marie instead. "Anne-Marie?"

"She took her own life," the woman whispered. "Andrew was devastated. I've never seen him so distraught. His father died when he was a boy, so his mother was all he had."

Daisy winced. "That's what I thought."

"What has that got to do with anything?" Mimi shook her head in confusion.

"Everything," Daisy replied. "Anne-Marie, where did you get your rings? Were they from her too?"

Anne-Marie stared at her. "Yes, she left them to me in her will, but how did you know?"

"I saw an article in a Scottish newspaper about how your mother-in-law lost everything, including her home."

Anne-Marie's face clouded over. "That's right. That scoundrel Macpherson totally destroyed her. She was destitute; she'd invested all of her savings into that scheme. We took her in, but she was too proud to live off the charity of others. She didn't want to be a burden. One night, she took an overdose of sleeping tablets. Andrew found her when he got home from work. She had drowned herself in the bathtub." Her voice shook. "It was a terrible time."

"It was the year after that when you saw Thomas Pierce in Edgemead, wasn't it? And you realized who he was?"

Floria and Mimi both stared at Anne-Marie, aghast. They were beginning to connect the dots.

Anne-Marie seemed unperturbed. "That's right. I couldn't believe my eyes when I spotted him. He'd left Scotland under a cloud of condemnation. There were a lot of angry people after him, but the police wouldn't prosecute. There wasn't enough evidence. Macpherson got himself a clever lawyer and managed to get off on minor charges. Then he skipped the country." She glared at Daisy. "All those lives ruined and he just skips off into the sunset with millions of pounds of stolen money. It's not right."

"Is that when you decided to take matters into your

own hands?" Daisy wondered how far away Josh was. If Anne-Marie decided to bolt, she wasn't sure they'd be able to catch her. By the looks of things, she wasn't armed. That was something, at least. "You lured him out here to Holly Lodge under the pretext of wanting to view the property, then killed him and hid his body up the chimney."

Anne-Marie wasn't a tall woman, but she was quite robust. She might have had the strength to shove Thomas into the chimney and board it up. McGuinness had been right. She'd been too hasty with her profile, even though statistically speaking the murderer was more likely to be a man. In this case, she'd been wrong.

But Anne-Marie was staring at her like she was mad. "What? No, of course I didn't kill him. I didn't like him, obviously, but I didn't want him dead."

"Don't lie to us, Anne-Marie. We know you called the agency and requested a viewing. You spoke to Thomas's colleague, Clive Collington, who gave you Thomas's number. After that, it was a simple matter of luring him here. What excuse did you give? An urgent cash sale? It would have had to be something enticing enough for him to stop by on his way to the Christmas charity bash."

"I'm sorry, Daisy, you've lost me." Anne-Marie stared at her, thoroughly confused. "I've never been to Holly Lodge before today. I didn't lure anyone here and I certainly didn't kill Thomas Macpherson."

Then the penny dropped. It wasn't Anne-Marie who was the killer, it was her husband, Andrew. He was Persephone's only son, and when she committed suicide, it sent him over the edge. Anne-Marie must have come to the same conclusion because her hand flew to her mouth. "No. It can't be."

They felt a cold draft and a male voice said, "Well, isn't this a nice little gathering? Darling, you should have told me you were meeting them here. I would have come with you."

Daisy didn't know what to do. Her mind had gone blank when she'd spotted the gun in Andrew's hand, and it was pointing right at them.

Chapter 22

"Andrew," Anne-Marie gasped. "What are you doing?"

"Something I should have done as soon as we arrived." His gaze turned to Daisy. "I knew you were bad news as soon as I met you. Interfering busybody."

"Please, Andrew. Put the gun down," Anne-Marie begged, but her husband ignored her. His focus was on Daisy.

Once she'd got over the initial shock of having a weapon pointed at her, Daisy said, "Anne-Marie told you about seeing Thomas in the High Street, didn't she? You couldn't believe your luck. You'd been searching for him for months and there he was, right on your doorstep."

Floria stared at Daisy as if she was mad. "Daisy, don't antagonize him. He's got a gun!" Mimi had gone white.

But Daisy knew she had to stall for time. Josh, and

hopefully the police, would be here soon. If she could keep him talking long enough, they might stand a chance.

Andrew sneered at her. "Damn right, I'd been searching for him. The bastard wrecked my mother's life. He took everything from her until the only way out was suicide. Why should he be allowed to live when he'd destroyed so many others?"

"You could have called the police," Daisy said, her eyes on the gun.

He scoffed. "And what would they have done? There were never any serious charges brought against him. The authorities didn't want to know."

"That's when you decided to go after him?"

"Of course. It's what anyone would have done." Daisy wasn't so sure about that, but she let him ramble on. "When Anne-Marie told me who she'd seen, I immediately went to look for him. I followed him to a charity shop in Esher. Pierce was a con man through and through. I knew he was using the charity to launder his blood money. My mother's money!"

"You went in looking for him?"

"Yes, I spoke to that stupid girl with the blue hair. She told me where he worked."

"Wendy," Daisy said quietly. "Her name was Wendy."

"Whatever." He shrugged and Daisy knew she was dealing with a sociopath. The man had no empathy whatsoever. Except for his mother, but that seemed to be rooted in anger, not love. He was filled with a need for vengeance.

"You called the agency and spoke to Clive?" Daisy pressed him to divulge more of the story. It was the only way she could keep him talking and prevent him from pulling that trigger. Where was Josh?

"He gave me Pierce's number. As soon as I spoke to the thieving devil, I knew he had to die."

Anne-Marie gave a low moan and swayed dangerously. She'd gone as gray as the peeling wallpaper around them. Floria reached out and took her arm, but she hardly noticed. She was staring at her husband like he was from outer space. Mimi stood silently at the back, her cat's eyes huge and terrified.

"You lured him here, to Holly Lodge, under the pretext of wanting to view the property."

He laughed. "It was so simple. I promised him a cash sale and because Pierce was always a greedy bastard, he jumped at the chance. Then he arrived dressed in that ridiculous Santa suit. He was going to some charity event." He snorted. "The idiot deserved what he got. I stuffed him up the chimney. Pretty fitting, don't you think?"

Anne-Marie's grip on Floria tightened. "How can you say that?" she hissed at her husband. "He was a bad man but he didn't deserve to die."

Andrew's attention swayed from Daisy to his wife. "I did what I had to do. He couldn't be allowed to get away with it. You weren't the one to find Mother in the bathtub. He killed her."

"I know, but murder?" She shook her head. "Oh, Andrew, what were you thinking?"

"You weren't thinking, were you, Andrew?" Daisy interjected. "You acted on instinct. You saw an opportunity to avenge your mother's death and you took it."

He snarled. "Damn right, I took it—and now you're going to die too, because you know too much." He leveled the gun at them.

"Andrew, no!" Anne-Marie broke free from Floria's grip and launched herself at him.

Daisy yelled at Floria and Mimi. "Run!"

They darted through the French doors that Floria had opened briefly to let some air into the place when they'd first arrived, and out into the garden. A shot ran out, followed by breaking glass. Andrew had fired right through the patio doors.

Anne-Marie screamed, and then there was a shout and Andrew appeared on the terrace. "Don't think you can get away, Daisy Thorne. You and your little friends are going down."

Mimi yelped as they dashed toward the bridge over the little stream. "It's broken," she warned as she jumped over it. Her long dancer's legs did a perfect split leap. Floria was ever-so slightly less elegant, while Daisy jumped over, her momentum propelling her forward. She fell onto her knees on the grass on the other side, but Floria helped her up.

Another shot pinged off the cobblestone bridge. He was close, but it was hard to hit a moving target, or so Daisy had been told, so she urged them to keep moving. "Come on, this way. Let's head for the meadow." There was a scattering of trees on the far side, which would give them some coverage.

But Andrew kept coming. There wasn't a peep from Anne-Marie and Daisy dreaded to think what he'd done to her. She glanced over her shoulder. He was at the bridge. He took a step onto the arch and there was a crunching sound like a mini-rockfall. He cried out in surprise as the bridge collapsed beneath his weight and he landed on his behind in the freezing stream with a splash.

"Aargh!" The angry yell frightened Daisy even more.

Now he was well and truly mad, but it had bought them some extra time. They heard tires crunching on the gravel outside. Thank goodness! Help had arrived, and not a moment too soon. Andrew was on his hands and knees searching beneath the water for his weapon, which he'd dropped in the fall.

"Hello?" called Josh, coming around the side of the house.

"Josh, out here!" screamed Floria, recognizing her husband's voice.

"Careful, he's got a gun!" Mimi yelled.

Josh immediately went into a crouch position as he scanned the garden for their assailant.

DCI McGuinness appeared on the terrace and with one look, realized what was happening. He took off toward the stream where Andrew, who had found his gun, was straightening up. Daisy saw him take aim.

"Get down," she yelled, as a shot went off. All three of them hit the grass.

Josh took off at a run, leaping over the fallen bridge with ease. "Floria!"

"Drop the weapon!" yelled McGuinness as he launched himself off the embankment and onto Andrew before he could get off another shot. The two men fell onto the shiny pebbles, icy water gushing over their bodies. McGuinness wrestled the shooter to the ground and bashed his hand holding the weapon onto some rocks until he released it.

"I said, Drop the weapon," he gritted, pulling Andrew's hands behind his back. With a grunt, Andrew went limp and McGuinness handcuffed him. Then he pulled the soaking gunman to his feet.

"Oh my gosh! Paul, are you okay?" Daisy ran to the

side of the stream. After that flying leap onto the gunman, she couldn't believe he wasn't injured.

"I'm fine." He grimaced, attempting to haul a bedraggled Andrew up the embankment. It was slippery and they stumbled several times. Andrew's hands were tied behind his back so he couldn't support himself and McGuinness was holding onto his captive, so he couldn't either. The gun was still in the stream.

Josh waded in and gave McGuinness a hand. They'd just got Andrew out when the cavalry arrived in a cacophony of screeching tires and blaring sirens. Several uniformed police officers burst out into the garden.

"Better late than never," Josh muttered. He put an arm around a relieved Floria and a shaken Mimi. "It's okay, you're safe now."

"Oh, thank goodness." Floria leaned into him.

McGuinness read Andrew his rights. "Andrew Williams, I'm arresting you for the murder of Thomas Pierce, the murder of Wendy Hayward, and the attempted murder of Daisy Thorne, Floria Graham, and Mimi Fallon." He handed the offender over to two policemen. "Take him back to Guildford and book him. I'll be there as soon as I can."

"Yes, sir." They led a dripping, fuming Andrew away. Another officer retrieved the weapon from the stream and placed it into a plastic evidence bag.

They went inside the lodge. A policewoman was attending to an ashen Anne-Marie, who was sitting on the floor bleeding from a head wound. Andrew must have hit her over the head with his gun. She appeared dazed, but it was difficult to know whether it was shock over her husband's actions or the concussion he'd given her.

"I'm sorry I suspected you." Daisy crouched down beside her. "It was the ring that helped me make the connection."

She grasped Daisy's hand. "I'm so sorry. My husband . . . what he did. It's unforgivable." She burst into tears.

The policewoman gave Daisy a look that said, *Can't this wait?*

Daisy stood up. McGuinness was talking to Josh, Floria, and Mimi. "I'm glad you're all okay. You did well to get away from that guy."

Floria held out a hand as Daisy approached. "It was thanks to Daisy here. She told us to run, otherwise I'm sure he would have shot us. He was quite mad." She took her friend's hand. "You were so brave."

Daisy grimaced. "I don't know about that. I stupidly accused Anne-Marie and then her husband walked in with that gun, surprising us."

"I thought he was going to kill us," breathed Mimi. "But you kept him talking, Daisy. I don't know how you had the guts to do that. I was shaking in my boots."

Daisy shrugged. "I had no choice. I knew that Josh and the police were coming because I'd called them on the way here. I just had to keep him from shooting us until they arrived."

"It's a good thing you did too," McGuinness remarked dryly. "A few moments later and who knows what might have happened."

"I'm so relieved you're okay." Josh gazed at his wife. "That was a close one."

Floria wrapped her arms around him. "We're safe now, thanks to you and DCI McGuinness. By the way, that was an impressive tackle, Paul," she told the detective, who was still dripping wet. He'd removed his heavy coat, but his shirt was sticking to his body and his hair was sticking up in all directions. Daisy thought so too. He'd launched himself off the bank like an action hero.

He grunted. "I had to take him down before he shot you."

"I hope he goes away for a long time." Mimi stared after the police, who were clearing out of the house, taking their prisoner and the gun with them.

McGuinness said, "There was DNA found beneath Wendy's fingernails, so hopefully that will link Andrew to her murder, but Thomas's body was too decomposed to get any real evidence from it."

"I have no doubt you'll get a full confession." Daisy met his gaze. The killer had been caught and she, Floria, and Mimi had survived unscathed, thanks to Josh's timely arrival and McGuinness's heroic actions.

"You can count on it. I will need a statement from all of you about what happened here. I want to add attempted murder to his rap sheet."

"I'll drive them to the police station," Josh said. "It's Christmas Eve, so we don't want to be gone too long."

"Yes, I've got to get home to prepare for tomorrow." Floria shot a pointed look at Daisy.

"How on earth did you know it was one of the Williamses?" McGuinness asked, as the paramedics helped Anne-Marie onto a stretcher.

"Her ring." Daisy pointed to the fake emerald on Anne-Marie's finger. "I Googled Thomas Macpherson's investment scam and saw that same ring on one of the victims. I knew then that there must be a connection between them."

He gazed at her in wonder. "I studied the list of victims and didn't make the link."

"You didn't know Anne-Marie and Andrew's last name," she pointed out.

"No, I've never met them before today."

"You couldn't have known they were related to one of the scam victims, Mrs. Persephone Williams, who committed suicide after she lost everything, including her home. After that, I raced out here to warn Floria and Mimi because I knew they were meeting with Anne-Marie to show her the house." She glanced at McGuinness's face. "I thought it was her and that I'd got the criminal profile wrong."

His voice softened. "No, you weren't wrong. Spot-on, in fact. It was a man, he wasn't from around here, but he'd visited in the past. I don't know what his occupation is, but I'll bet it's got something to do with construction."

"He's a carpenter," said Anne-Marie, as they wheeled her out on a stretcher. "He makes bespoke furniture for a kitchen company."

"There you go." McGuinness's gaze lingered on Daisy. "You never cease to amaze me, Miss Thorne."

Floria winked at her.

"Now all that's left is to find the missing money," Mimi said. "Then this case will be closed and we can go back to renovating our house."

Daisy gasped. In all the chaos, she'd completely forgotten to mention it. "Actually, I think I know where it is."

Chapter 23

Everyone stared at her.

"You do?" McGuinness uttered.

"Where?" Mimi asked. "We searched the whole place from top to bottom the other day. It's not here."

"It was something Krish said." Her eyes glittered. "It didn't click immediately, but when I was thinking about it earlier today, it suddenly came to me."

"Is it here?" Floria demanded, looking around her.

"I think so."

"What money?" Josh asked.

Floria squeezed his arm. "The money Thomas Pierce stole from all the people he swindled up in Scotland."

Josh frowned. "The dead guy?"

"Yes." Daisy snorted. "He wasn't a very nice man."

"That's putting it mildly," grunted McGuinness. "Daisy, where is this hidden stash?"

"Follow me." She led them into the dilapidated kitchen with its wonky table, peeling wallpaper, and faded linoleum tiles. The sun was setting and it was getting dark, so Josh switched on the light. Daisy walked over to the boiler cupboard. "It struck me as odd that the boiler didn't work. It was totally dead when we tried it before."

"It has been several years since it was operational," pointed out Josh.

"Yes, but even the power to it had been turned off."

"That's right," said Mimi, her green eyes flashing with anticipation. "It was freezing in here the other day and we couldn't switch it on."

McGuinness stood beside Daisy. He reached in and flicked the power switch, but nothing happened. "She's right," he said. "The electricity isn't on to this particular unit."

"There's an electric box in the hall," said Mimi helpfully. "Maybe the switch has tripped."

"Unlikely," said McGuinness. "It's been disconnected." He held up a loose wire. "Somebody's deliberately sabotaged it. This is a clean cut."

"That's because there's something in here," Daisy said.

"Do you think so?" gasped Floria.

"He hid the money in the boiler?" Josh raised his eyebrows.

McGuinness, who was nice and tall, stood on his toes and pried the lid off the boiler. It was rusty and the metal grated as he heaved. Eventually, it came off.

"I can't see inside," he muttered, looking around for something to stand on.

"Here, use this chair," said Josh, sliding it toward him.

"Careful, they're a bit wobbly," Mimi pointed out.

Daisy got out the way so Josh could hold the chair while McGuinness climbed up to have a look inside the boiler. He peered over the top, frowned, then reached inside. They all held their breath. He made a triumphant sound and pulled out a large, black refuse bag.

"You've found it!" gasped Daisy.

Floria clapped her hands together. "Gosh, this is so exciting. It's like finding buried treasure."

"In my house," added Mimi.

He laid it on the table and brushed off the dust and cobwebs. It was the moment of truth. Daisy's heart pounded as she stared at their find.

"Do you want to do the honors?" McGuinness asked her.

She hesitated. "Can I?"

"Of course."

"It was you who found it, Dais," said Floria.

"Okay." Daisy tentatively reached for the bag. A small insect scuttled away as she undid the tie at the top. It was pretty well secured and it took her a few minutes to undo the knot. Eventually, it gave way and she peered inside. Her eyes widened. "Wow. I can see why he wanted to keep this hidden."

"Let's see," begged Floria. All four of their heads were leaning forward to get a glimpse.

Daisy upended the bag and wads of fifty-pound notes

secured together by elastic bands fell out onto the table. They all stared in awe.

"There must be at least a hundred bundles here," muttered McGuinness, picking up one of them to inspect it. Josh, who was a finance whiz, did the same. "I'd guess these are ten-thousand pound bundles," he said, doing a quick calculation. "That means if there are a hundred wads, there is a million pounds in that bag."

"A million pounds," murmured Floria, staring at the pile on the kitchen table. "That's a lot of money."

"Worth killing for," added Daisy.

Mimi gave a low whistle.

"The funny thing is," said Daisy, "when Andrew lured him here to kill him, he had no idea the cash was only meters away."

McGuinness looked up. "For Andrew, it wasn't about the money. He murdered Thomas to avenge his mother's death. I doubt he even considered the money."

"He probably figured it was long gone," said Floria. "It had been some time since the scam in Scotland."

Mimi flopped back in her chair. "I'm just glad this is all over now and I can get back to finishing my house."

"Holly Lodge finally gave up her secret," mused Daisy.

McGuinness began putting the money back into the bag. "I'll have to take this with me as evidence," he said. "Once we've processed it for prints, the Scottish authorities can redistribute it to the victims of Thomas Macpherson's scheme."

"At least some good came out of it," said Daisy. "Although it's too late for Persephone Williams, unfortunately."

Once McGuinness had repacked the bag, they all walked out front. The snowy drive had been churned up by all the emergency vehicles, but the house still looked picture-perfect with its snowy roof and pretty holly bushes.

"Well, that was an interesting afternoon." Josh beeped his key ring to unlock his SUV. "But I'm glad it's over and no one was hurt." He opened the passenger door for his wife.

"Do you want to come with us to the police station," Floria asked Daisy.

She shook her head. "I've got my car so I'll meet you there."

Floria flashed her a knowing grin and climbed into the passenger seat. Mimi got in the back.

"I don't know how you do it," McGuinness said. "Somehow, you always manage to figure it out before I do. If this carries on, I'll be out of a job."

Daisy laughed. "I doubt that, but we do make a good team."

His voice deepened. "That we do."

There was a short pause, then he said, "Look, I've got to go. They're waiting for me at the station."

"Yes, of course. If I don't see you there, good luck with the interrogation." She knew he'd have his hands full interviewing and charging Andrew Williams.

His eyes blazed into hers, then he gave a curt nod and turned away.

"Paul?" she called after him.

He turned around. "Yes?"

"Will you come with me to Floria's Christmas lunch tomorrow? If you don't already have plans, that is?"

His face relaxed into a smile. "As it turns out, my current investigation is about to be wrapped up, so I have some free time on my hands."

Daisy's stomach fluttered. "Is that a yes?"

His eyes twinkled. "That's a definite yes."

Chapter 24

They all crowded into the dining room at Brompton Court.

"The house looks incredible," Daisy told Floria. Fairy lights twinkled on the portico outside, as well as around the banister of the grand staircase to where Dame Serena's picture hung majestically at the top. Was it Daisy's imagination or was the glint in her eyes softer now than it had been before as she looked down on her family gathered together?

Floria sparkled in a sequined blue top as she flitted around, making sure everyone had a drink in their hand. Josh barely left her side. Donna was the picture of understated elegance in a dove-gray knitted dress that clung to her body in all the right places and looked wonderful with her dark, smoky hair and witchy green eyes. She and her husband Greg had been filled in on the events of the last few days and couldn't believe what had transpired. "I'm so glad you weren't hurt?" she said, glancing worriedly at her sisters. "That man sounds quite demented."

"I think seeing Thomas Pierce again pushed him over the edge," Daisy told them. "Anne-Marie said he never used to be aggressive until his mother died, and then it was as if he'd turned into a different person."

"Even so, she never believed him capable of murder," Floria added. She'd visited Anne-Marie in hospital where she was being kept for observation.

Mimi shivered. "Imagine finding out your husband is a killer?"

Rob, her husband, leaned across and kissed her on the cheek. "Let's not dwell on it," he said. "It's Christmas."

"Agreed," said Daisy, admiring her date. Paul had picked her up at her cottage so they could arrive at Brompton Court together. He looked smarter than she'd ever seen him, in a dark gray suit with a black shirt, open at the neck. It matched his eyes that glittered with good humor. On his shirtsleeves were the silver police handcuff cuff links she'd bought him. It was a fun gift, nothing serious. He, on the other hand, had got her a lovely pair of daisy-shaped earrings, also in sterling silver and decorated with glittering cubic zirconia stones. She absolutely loved them.

Now the case was wrapped up, the tension in his neck and shoulders had disappeared, and he seemed very much at ease, laughing and joking with her friends. It was hard to believe this was the same man who stared down and arrested hardened criminals.

"Did Andrew Williams confess?" Josh wanted to know.

"He did. There was no point in holding anything back since he'd been caught red-handed, so to speak. He even admitted to strangling Wendy at the market. I think he was proud of the fact. He wanted people to know what he'd done."

"Certifiable," Floria said, shivering. "I could see he'd lost the plot as soon as he walked in holding that gun. There was something demented in his eyes, like he wasn't quite there."

"Yes, he thinks he's avenged his mother's death." McGuinness shook his head.

"How sad," Donna remarked. "Now he'll spend the rest of his life in prison."

"With a bit of luck," McGuinness added. "The skin samples under Wendy's fingernails matched his DNA, so he was charged with both murders, not to mention the attempted murder of Daisy, Floria, and Mimi."

Mimi reached for her wine. "I've never had a gun pointed at me before. It was terrifying."

"Let's hope it was the first and last time," muttered Rob.

"Your statements helped," McGuinness said. "Along with the gun that he'd purchased illegally from an ex-con. It had been used in a previous homicide, according to the ballistics report, so we've nabbed that guy too."

"All in all a successful outcome," said Floria.

"What happened to Bas Lightman?" Daisy asked.

"He narrowly escaped jail by agreeing to pay back every penny Thomas Pierce donated to the charity, plus interest. And Hannah Collington has turned over the funds in her account that were plundered from the investment scheme. She wanted nothing to do with it. It looks like the people who were flounced will get their money back, or at least some form of compensation."

"That's great," said Daisy. "Some good came out of it in the end."

"It's Anne-Marie I feel sorry for." Floria grimaced. "She's all alone in the hospital."

"Is she all right?" Mimi asked.

"Yes, I think so. She has a concussion—Andrew hit her rather hard—but she'll survive. It's still a shock."

"Of course," said Daisy. How could it not be? Her husband had murdered two people and held a gun on them.

"I've been giving it a lot of thought, and I've decided to sell Brompton Court to her," Floria told her guests.

"Oh no," whispered Donna. "You love this place."

"It was a tough decision to make." Josh placed a hand over Floria's.

Floria's eyes were bright. "It's time. We can't afford to keep it going. A manor house this size costs an absolute fortune to run, and Violeta and Pepe want to retire. I can't expect them to stay here and run it. Josh and I won't be using it."

"It seems such a shame to let it go," mused Daisy. The decadent glamour of Serena's parties was something she'd never forget.

"I know, but I didn't have particularly happy memories here and even if Josh and I did move back to Edgemead one day, we wouldn't want to stay in a twelve-bedroom mansion like this. It's too big for us."

"Mimi has given me an idea," said Rob. Everybody turned to him. "It needs a bit of ironing out, but it is possible that my company, the Fallon Hotel Group, may be able to purchase Brompton Court to add to its premier collection."

Floria gasped. "Really? You'd consider buying it?"

Mimi took her sister's hand. "It would keep it in the family."

Rob continued, "I've been looking for another project in the UK since Mimi is going to be spending so much time here, and this would be perfect for our portfolio. I'll have to run it by the board, of course, but I can't see how they'd refuse. It's in a pristine location; it's got twelve bedrooms and ample land for amenities. It would make a perfect wedding destination. We could even build a nine-hole golf course and a swimming pool. Perhaps even a spa."

"Wow, this is a lot to take in," said Floria, her eyes gleaming. "I'd love it if you bought it, Rob. I know you'd keep its original character and grandeur."

"Of course he would." Mimi glowed as she looked at her husband. "And more importantly, if you didn't want to sell it outright, you could be a silent partner. That way you'd still own a share of your family legacy."

"I don't know what to say." Floria's eyes filled with tears.

"Say yes," urged Rob. "I'll get an architect to work on some designs with me over the next few weeks and I'll run it past the board when I fly back to Australia in mid-January. Can you hold off signing it over to the National Trust until then?"

"Absolutely!" Floria jumped up and gave him a hug. "Oh, I can't believe this. I'm so happy."

"It's the perfect solution," agreed Daisy.

"It also means I have an excuse to be here to supervise the sale and refurbishment," said Rob. Mimi shot a sly glance at Floria. "I had a vested interest. I get to have my husband close by while I'm on tour."

"This is cause for celebration," said Greg, reaching for the champagne.

Josh stood up. "Since we're celebrating, there's something else Floria and I want to share with you all."

All eyes turned to him. He took Floria's hand and grinned around the table. "My lovely wife and I are expecting."

"Oh my goodness!" Mimi jumped out of her chair to hug her. "You should have said something earlier. How long have you known?"

"We wanted to wait the obligatory twelve weeks before we announced it," she said. "But then with everything that happened at Holly Lodge, it didn't seem like the right time."

"Congratulations." Daisy couldn't have been happier for her friend.

Josh was beaming from ear to ear. "Thanks, we can't wait for the little guy to arrive."

"Or girl," corrected Floria. Her husband winked at her. It was clear he was overjoyed.

"That's wonderful," said Donna rather wistfully. Greg put a hand on her leg and Daisy thought she saw a look pass between them. Were they trying for a baby too?

She smiled around at her friends. What could be a better Christmas gift than the promise of a new life? "Let's have a toast," she said, holding up her glass. "To new beginnings."

"To new beginnings," they all chanted in unison.

"And to family and friendship," added Floria.

"To family and friendship," they echoed. Everyone clinked glasses and took a sip of their champagne.

"Cheers." Daisy turned to McGuinness to find his eyes on her.

"To new beginnings," he said softly. She felt a warmth spread over her that had nothing to do with the champagne.

"To new beginnings."

There was a lot to be grateful for this Christmas.

Did you miss the fun of the first Daisy Thorne mystery?
No worries! Keep reading to enjoy the opening chapter
of *Death at a Country Mansion* . . . available from
Kensington Publishing Corp.

Chapter One

The ice in her glass tinkled provocatively as the scotch hit it. Another marriage in tatters. Her fourth, in fact. Serena shook her head and took a big gulp, feeling the whiskey encase her in a golden glow as it went down. Bastard. How could Collin do this to her? With an air hostess, of all people. What the hell was he thinking?

She'd arrived home earlier that afternoon to find her husband packing. The lunch meeting with her solicitor had finished earlier than expected; otherwise she'd never have caught him.

"I'm leaving you, Serena." He tossed shorts and T-shirts into his suitcase, then fumbled in his dresser for the sunscreen. "I wanted to avoid a confrontation, but you're here, so you may as well hear it from me. You're a drunk. You've made my life intolerable. I've had it with your bitching and sniping, not to mention your blatant attempts to seduce every red-blooded man who walks through the door. Christ, you're an embarrassment."

She'd been so stunned; she hadn't known how to respond. Yes, her drinking had gotten out of hand lately, and she had tried to chat up that handsome, young musician at the summer party, but that was Collin's fault for ignoring her. What did he expect her to do? He certainly didn't touch her anymore.

He continued, "I've met someone, someone who appreciates me. We're going to the house in the Bahamas. My solicitor will be in touch." Collin hauled the heavy suitcase onto the landing. It was the beige one, the same one he'd had on their honeymoon.

Feeling a surge of rage, she'd stumbled after him. "What do you mean you've met someone? Who?"

"None of your business."

"What do you mean it's none of my business? You're my husband, for Christ's sake. Who is she?" She was screeching now, a horrid, high-pitched sound tinged with desperation.

"If you must know, her name is Bernadette, and she's an air hostess. We met on my last trip to Paris."

Serena stared at him. This couldn't be happening. "How dare you walk out on me! And that's my house in the Bahamas. I bought it and I forbid you to use it as a sordid shag pad." Her voice rose hysterically, as it often did when she'd been drinking, and she'd had a bottle of sauvignon blanc with lunch.

He turned to face her, his voice unusually calm. Normally, they'd both be screaming at each other by now. "That's rich, coming from you. And for your information, we put the Nassau house in my name, remember? For tax purposes. It's mine now." He smirked and picked up the suitcase to carry it downstairs.

The grand staircase was Serena's favorite feature in the stately old mansion, and the main reason she'd bought it almost three decades before. It seemed like a lifetime. She adored the glorious mahogany balustrade with spiral spindles that Violeta, the housekeeper, kept polished to a high shine, and the soft lilac carpeting with gold strips. It reminded her of elegant Venetian palaces and old-fashioned grandeur. She'd once performed for a select group of guests, standing at the top of the grand staircase. The rapture on their faces as she sung Puccini's "O Mio Babbino Caro" had made her heart soar.

Serena floundered after him, coming to an unsteady halt on the landing. "Please, Collin, don't do this. Let's talk about it."

He'd glanced up, but instead of looking at her, his gaze rose to the portrait of the woman she'd once been, which hung above her head. That's when she knew it was truly over. He couldn't even look at her anymore. She turned up her face to the painting, grasping the balustrade so as not to lose her balance. It had been commissioned at the height of her fame, and the beautiful, serene expression on her face made her heart twist every time she saw it. She'd been so happy then. Life had been magical. Her records were selling, her concerts were sold out, everyone wanted a piece of her. How had it all gone so wrong?

"I didn't want it to end like this, you know." Collin's face softened momentarily. "But you left me no choice. Living with you has become . . . impossible."

At that point, she'd fallen to her knees, tears streaming down her face.

"I hope you find some peace, Serena."

And he walked out of the house, pulling his suitcase behind him.

Serena hung her head and sobbed, great rasping sounds that resonated from the depths of her soul. The hand holding the tumbler drooped, spilling the drink on the Persian rug. She didn't care. How had her life come to this?

Age was a bitch. Once she'd hit fifty, her voice had gone downhill, no doubt helped along by the booze and the screaming matches with her husband. But without her singing, she was nothing, just an empty shell, and no matter how much she drank or how many lovers she took, she couldn't fill the void. Her laser-sharp soprano voice, which had once captivated the masses and enthralled-royalty, was no more. She'd lost that iridescent quality that allowed her to scale the fearsome heights of the most physically demanding music. She poured another drink, then another. Eventually, the sought-after haze descended and her head lolled back onto the headrest of the chaise longue.

Serena woke with a start in the middle of the night and looked around in a panic. Where was she? Oh, yeah. She was still on the chaise longue, fully clothed.

What was that noise that had woken her? Was it the front door? She listened, holding her breath. The room swam in front of her eyes and her tongue was parched. A wave of nausea hit her and she bent over, fearing she might be sick. God, she'd polished off most of the scotch. That was heavy, even for her. There was a loud creak on the staircase. She recognized it. The loose board before the landing.

Someone was in the house.

She glanced around for a weapon, but all she could find was the empty whiskey bottle on the side table. Grabbing it by the neck, she stumbled toward the door. Her heart pounded as she peered onto the landing.

Relief flooded her body. "Oh, thank God, it's you. You almost gave me a heart attack."

She dropped her arm carrying the bottle, just as the intruder raised his.

Serena screamed as she realized what was happening. Then came the hammer blow. Her head exploded in pain and she fell to her knees. The room spun, she was so dizzy.

"Why?" She reached out, trying to grab something, anything to stabilize herself. Her hand folded around the balustrade.

The intruder lifted her to her feet, and for a moment she thought it might be okay, but then he bent her over the railing. Her hand tightened its grip as she flopped forward.

"No, please . . ."

The intruder pried her fingers loose. It wasn't hard; she had no strength left. Then she felt herself falling. It was a strange sensation, and for a fleeting moment she felt weightless and free. Then the air was knocked out of her and darkness descended.

Connect with 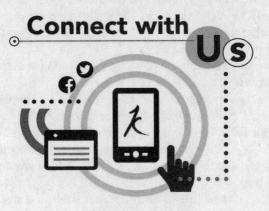Us

Visit us online at
KensingtonBooks.com
to read more from your favorite authors, see books
by series, view reading group guides, and more.

Join us on social media

for sneak peeks, chances to win books and prize packs,
and to share your thoughts with other readers.

facebook.com/kensingtonpublishing
twitter.com/kensingtonbooks

Tell us what you think!

To share your thoughts, submit a review,
or sign up for our eNewsletters, please visit:
KensingtonBooks.com/TellUs.